Follow Your Heart

Follow Your Heart

Jacqueline M. Ryan

Enjoy!

Jacqueline M. Ryan

Follow Your Heart

Create Space,
100 Enterprise Way, Suite A200
Scotts Valley, CA 95066
USA

This is a work of fiction. All the characters, names, incidents, organizations, and dialogue in this novel are either the products of the author's imagination or are used fictitiously.

ISBN: 9781441401274
Printed in the United States of America

For my favorite Canadians:

Amanda, Afua, and Rebecca

Author's Note:

10% of the sales of Follow Your Heart will go to

The Leukemia and Lymphoma Society of America.

Enjoy your book knowing

you have helped in the fight against blood cancers.

Chapter One

♥

I looked around the townhouse one last time. I had packed up the last few things that were mine and put them in a box. I put the box down on the front porch. I left the keys on the small dining room table. It stung to look at the tastefully decorated living room that I had worked so hard to make comfortable, but I had to remind myself that this was not the end of my world. I closed the door to the townhouse and picked up the box. I walked to my car getting ready to drive away.

I thought about the decision to leave. I had made it. He had said I could stay at the house as long as I wanted, but I knew that would be a mistake. There were too many memories and now too much pain. If I was going to make life in Boston work, I was going to have to set out on my own. It was a tough decision, but one that I was sure would bring me the happiness I had sought by coming here.

I had just finished my master's degree in public relations at DePaul University in Chicago when I met Patrick O'Malley. He was so charming. He was just over six feet tall with brown hair with auburn and blond highlights. He was athletic but not overly muscular. And he had swept me off my feet. I had been twenty-three years old and so very naïve. When he had been transferred from Chicago to Boston, he had asked me if I had wanted to move with him. I had made stipulations. I would have my own apartment. I wasn't going to live with him. He had agreed, but I hadn't counted on the real estate market in Boston. Everything had been so expensive and I wasn't making nearly enough money. So one year later after trying to live with roommates I didn't know, I gave up and moved in with Patrick. After the second year our romantic relationship was over.

Here I was sitting in my Saab convertible, a graduation gift from my parents, with what was left of my things piled in the back seat of the car. My father had worked for General Motors and had secured a great price for my Saab. I backed up and headed out of the parking lot swearing to never look back. I was determined to look forward. I had leased a small apartment in Cambridge, Massachusetts; a month-to-month rental. I was still looking for something permanent that was close to work. It was small, but it was mine. Everything in it was mine. When I had moved to Boston I had difficulty finding a job in public relations. Sure there were jobs, but no one wanted to deal with my visa. The ones that agreed to hire me blatantly lied about the job requirements. I hadn't realized that would be such a problem. Canadians working in Chicago was a regular occurrence. Boston's tight job market and companies' ignorance of the process kept me from getting many of the coveted jobs. I finally secured at job at University of Massachusetts Hospital in the public relations department.

I loved working at the hospital. The pay wasn't too bad and the work was so rewarding. I loved going up to the pediatric ward to see the kids. The hours were demanding but there were perks involved. Many of the local sports teams would send representatives to the hospitals. Many times, they would leave tickets for the staff. I had always been an avid sports fan and my insatiable desire to see a live game was met by my job.

The hospital had its down side too. I was on call every third weekend. I was one of three public relations officers under the Head of Public Relations. At twenty-five I was considered too young for that job. I hoped if I did my time and paid my dues, I would be promoted from within when the job opened up. The Head of PR, Mr. Ezekiel Roberts, was an elderly man who really shouldn't be running the PR department for a major hospital any longer. There were many things he shouldn't be doing but he was well connected, so he stayed on. I could only hope for his retirement.

My cell phone began to ring as I was heading up I93 toward my apartment. The caller ID said it was the hospital.

"Hello?" I answered.

"Diana, am I glad to get you!" It was Dr. Henry, head of the Emergency Room, "We have a problem. Mr. Roberts hit a pedestrian on Washington Street this afternoon. We need you at the hospital immediately for a press conference."

"No problem," I said and hung up the phone. I got off the highway and made my way to the hospital. At the employee garage, George waved me through.

"Thanks George," I waved back. I parked and locked my car. I headed into the building. I always kept a spare set of clothes in my office for problems like this. I ran to my office and closed the door. I quickly changed clothes and headed down to the Emergency Room.

There was already a crowd of reporters outside the ER door. "Great." I muttered looking for Dr. Henry. I found him at the main doctor and nurses' station.

"What's going on?" I asked Dr. Henry.

"Hi Diana," Dr. Henry said taking off his glasses. "So you're on call this weekend."

"Just my luck. Tell me what happened."

"Apparently Mr. Roberts was driving down Washington Street and hit a young man in his thirties. Apparently, the young man was slightly injured. He broke his left arm and has a slight concussion. The problem is not the victim, it is Mr. Roberts."

"What's the problem?" I asked.

"He had a heart attack on the scene and couldn't be revived in time. He's in a coma right now and there doesn't seem to be much hope that he will come out of it."

My jaw dropped.

"This is despite the efforts of the victim who is a pediatrician from North Andover," he continued.

"Is the victim still in the ER?" I asked.

"Yeah. He's in one of the private exam rooms in the back."

Dr. Henry began leading me toward one of the back rooms. "They just finished setting his arm. He's bound to be in a great mood. Do you want to meet him?"

"Yeah. What's his name?" I asked.

"Dr. Steven Edwards."

Chapter Two

I was about to do something I swore I wouldn't do. I was about to interfere in Chelsea's life. I had moved to the Boston area in June and she had refused to move with me. I couldn't blame her. I had offered to marry her and she had refused. She had too much to sort out on her own. We had a relationship of convenience but I had grown to love her. I knew her feelings weren't reciprocal but I felt the need to give her some of the happiness she needed. We agreed to stay friends. After all, her brother Tommy was my best friend from college. It was Tommy that was our common bond and it was Tommy who was asking me to go back on my word.

The phone rang on Thursday night. I had just come home from the office. I saw it was Tommy on the caller ID.

"Hey, what's up?" I said as I sat down and pressed mute on the Celtics' game.

"Not much. How's Bean Town?" Tommy asked.

"Quiet now that baseball season is over. I can't even begin to understand the Red Sox fans. They are so obnoxious."

"Listen," Tommy, a New York City Firefighter and not one for small talk, started, "I have a favor to ask."

"Sure, what is it?" I asked.

"Chelsea's coming to town tomorrow. She has a signing at Barnes and Noble on Saturday."

"Tommy," I warned, "you know it didn't work out. We're both better off this way."

"I know. I know," he sighed. "She's not alone this weekend. I need you to check up on her."

"What do you mean she's not alone?" I asked.

"She's with her ex-boyfriend," he explained. "The one from college."

"Payne?" I asked standing up.

"Yeah," he said sheepishly. "They started seeing each other again a few weeks ago. I need you to check it out for me."

"I don't know Tommy," I said walking to the kitchen and grabbing a beer. "I promised her I wouldn't interfere in her life. We agreed to move on."

"Steve," Tommy began, "I need to know he's not going to hurt her again. I was upfront with him. I threatened to kill him if he hurt her. I'm afraid I'll never see the real Payne. Just go check it out."

"Fine." I agreed begrudgingly. "Where is she staying?"

"The Long Warf Marriott in Boston," Tommy offered.

"Fine. I'll go see her tomorrow night when she checks in."

"Thanks, Steve. I owe you one."

I hung up the phone. He would *so* owe me if this went south. I would look like the biggest loser on the face of the earth.

Friday, I put a long day in at the office. I took the train into Boston from my office in Lawrence. I wasn't too happy about doing this, but Tommy and I went way back. We met at Fordham University in the Bronx. Although we both grew up in New York, we hadn't crossed paths. Tommy had gone to Cathedral High School, a Catholic school for boys in Queens while I lived just over the border from Queens in Nassau County and had gone to Chamanade, another all boys' Catholic school. We bonded at Fordham despite the fact that our majors were so completely different. I was pre-med and Tommy was an economics major. The funny part was that Tommy ended up working for the Fire Department instead of doing anything with economics. I hoped that he would one day be made commissioner. He would know the economic side as well as the personnel side.

It had been a long day at the office. I had bought into a practice in Lawrence, Massachusetts. I wasn't going to get rich with a practice in Lawrence, but I felt like I was doing something constructive. Many of the residents were low-income working class families. Lawrence was one of the mill towns of the early 1800s that had fallen on hard times since manufacturing went overseas. Friday saw me ordering a battery of tests at UMASS General in Boston for a little boy. I was almost positive that he had leukemia. I had tried to prepare his parents for the eventual diagnosis and it had broken my heart. He would be checking in on Monday for the tests. I hoped I was wrong, but there wasn't much doubt in my mind.

It was almost seven when I arrived in Boston. I grabbed a bite to eat and a drink at the Purple Shamrock. It was around 8:30 when I walked over to the Long Warf Marriott. I went up to the desk and asked for Chelsea Michael's room.

"She's not registered here," the clerk said. "These flowers arrived earlier for her and we're not sure what to do with them. Is it possible that she is checking in with someone else?"

I nodded and wondered at the dozen roses. I looked at the envelope and tried to sneak a peek at whom they were from. I thought I saw "Love, Steve" written on the card. Silently, I cursed Tommy. He was interfering. Around nine, I saw Chelsea walk in with a tall slim man. I had forgotten how breathtakingly beautiful she was. She had long auburn hair with an hourglass figure that most women saw plastic surgeons to achieve. She was five foot eight but the man with her was taller. He was carrying two garment bags and went up to the desk.

He said something and nodded at the flowers.

Chelsea opened the envelope and lost some color in her face. She put the card back in the envelope and smiled at the man. I got up and was walking toward them.

"Who are they from?" I heard the man ask.

"No one," she said, "Is our room ready?"

"Chelsea," he warned, "who are they from?"

"They're from me," I answered. If possible, her face was even paler. She closed her eyes and shook her head.

"Dr. Steven Edwards," I said putting out my hand for him to shake.

He shook my hand, "Payne Williams." Chelsea finally looked up at me with a taut smile on her face.

"Hi Steve," she said not moving to shake my hand or embrace me in any way.

I leaned forward and kissed her cheek, "Happy Birthday Chelsea."

"Thanks. How did you know I was here?"

"I knew you had a signing at the Barnes and Noble. I asked Tommy where you were staying. When the florist said you didn't have a room here I decided to come over and wait." I was surprised I could lie that well. I needed to have a long talk with Tommy. She was less than thrilled to see me and the situation was very uncomfortable.

"Well, thanks for coming, but I'm booked pretty solid this weekend," she said giving me the cold shoulder. "Maybe next time you're in New York you can give us a call."

She turned and walked away with the room key in her hand leaving me alone with Payne. The flowers lay unclaimed on the counter. Payne picked up his garment bag and overnight case in preparation to follow her.

"Well then. It was nice to meet you," he said to me. "I really think it would be best if you left her alone. She's moved on and if you really cared about her, you'd let her go."

As he walked away, I shook my head. Tommy was in so much trouble with me. I was furious with him. He set me up in the worst way. I stormed out of the Marriott and made my way to Quincy Market. I took out my cell phone and called Tommy. His cell went right to his voice mail. If he knew what was good for him, he wouldn't answer his phone for a few days.

"Tommy," I said clipped. "What the fuck were you thinking sending flowers with my name on them? We need to talk about this. Call me."

I took the train home to North Andover. I had just purchased a house in the town. It wasn't too far of a drive from my house to the office.

Against my better judgment, I wanted to explain things to Chelsea. I figured the best place to do that was at the Barnes and Noble. Saturday morning I made my way downtown to The Barnes and Noble on Washington Street.

I walked in the door and immediately saw Chelsea. She was sitting at a table with a line of people waiting to have their books signed. She looked up as I came in the door and I met her eye. Before I knew it Payne was in front of me.

Payne approached me "Could I have a word with you in private?"

"Sure," I said following him into the alcove by the bathrooms.

"I really thought that I had made myself clear last night when I told you to let go." He was less than pleasant in his tone. That set me off. I didn't like being bullied around. Especially by this guy. I knew too much about him.

"I understand, but you have to know what she is like. I'm not about to give up without a fight. Is that what you're spoiling for? A fight?" I said.

"I really don't want to be that juvenile about it." He retorted. "As for knowing what she is like, I've known Chelsea ten years and I know more about her than you do."

"Do you?" I said getting angry, "Do you really?"

"Yeah I do," he said getting just as angry. "She loves me."

"Sure she does. She's loved you since she first met you and you left her. You left her alone and pregnant. She was so alone she tried to kill herself, not once but twice." As soon as I said it I regretted it. She had told me he never knew about the baby. The color drained from his face. Apparently she still hadn't told him.

"What! What are you talking about? She wasn't pregnant. She'd been on the pill for almost two years. She accidentally overdosed on sleeping pills one night."

"So you know her do you? Do you know she miscarried the baby the night she overdosed? Do you know what day that was? It was October sixteenth. A year ago, seven years later, that same day, she came home drunk and fell in bed with me. I held her that night while she cried. And where were you the last seven years when she was tortured once a year by her loss?"

He seemed struck by this information. He was silent while I continued. As long as everything was out on the table, I felt the need to let him know.

"So you listen to me," I continued, "Tommy doesn't know about the baby. As much as I'd love to tell him which would lead to the beating you so deserve, she loves you too much. And I can't understand why. She drove five hours to talk to you about the baby only to find out you were screwing someone else. She came home and drank herself into oblivion. Then there was the overdose and the miscarriage. So *you* know her? She never told you. But she told *me*."

"I'm back to stay Steve. I'm going to make it right. I'm going to marry her. Not because I feel sorry for her but because I love her. And she loves me."

"Has she told you she loves you?" I asked. From the look on his face I knew the answer. "I didn't think so. She can't say it. Don't expect her to say it because she told me she would never say it again. Ever. Tommy told me he already threatened your life. Let me make myself really clear. What Tommy will do to you won't even come close to what I'll do to you if you break her heart again."

I walked away from Payne careful not to look at Chelsea. I walked out the door. I felt horrible. This whole thing had gone so very badly. I had broken a rule. I had interfered and I had divulged information that Chelsea trusted me with. No one knew about her miscarriage. I had promised not to say anything, but I had been so filled with ire that I just told him. I was so lost in my own tortured existence that I didn't hear the car horn. I just felt the impact of the car as I fell to the ground. An elderly man was out of the car and standing over me; He was on his cell phone calling for an ambulance when I passed out.

Chapter Three

♥

I knocked lightly on the door to the private exam room. The private exam rooms were kept for the high profile clients of the hospitals. At any given time you could see a famous sports figure, an actor or a Kennedy cousin in any one of these rooms.

"Come in," I heard the man beckon.

I walked in to see the patient sitting on the stretcher with his left arm in a cast. His blond head was bent reading his own chart. He looked up when I came into the room. He had the most unbelievable blue eyes. It was like a live Ken doll.

"Dr. Edwards?" I asked as I stepped forward.

"Yes." He replied looking at me. I had changed into my black pants suit with a cream colored blouse unbuttoned to reveal my black tank top.

"My name's Diana Goyeau. I'm from the hospital's Public Relations department." I offered my hand to him.

He took it and shook it, "I'd really love to get out of here sometime soon Ms. Goyeau. It hasn't been my best day."

"Yeah. I'm sorry about that. Apparently it hasn't been a good day for quite a few people today." I said with a smile.

"How is Mr. Roberts?" He asked.

"I think perhaps its safe to say he's having the worst day out of all of us. Mr. Roberts has slipped into a coma. That's what I am here to talk to you about."

"Damn," he said rubbing his eyes with his right hand. "What's his prognosis?"

"I'm afraid not good," I answered. "That's where I come in."

"How's that?" He asked studying me.

"I'm here to hold the press conference that releases the details of the accident. The hospital would like you to appear at the press conference with Dr. Henry and me."

"I really would rather not do that," he insisted. "It's been a really bad day and I'd just rather get home and rest. I'm fairly certain the pain medication they gave me should be in effect until I get home."

"I understand that sir, but I really must insist that you stay for the press conference. You don't have to say anything. You can just sit up front."

"And if I don't stay?" He looked at me suspiciously

"I'm sorry to say that the press may follow you back to your house in North Andover and you wouldn't get the rest you so want." I smiled at him sweetly.

He whistled, "You know how to play hardball."

"Comes from having two older brothers. You can rest in here and I will come get you in about a half an hour for the conference. Can I get you anything before the news conference?"

"I'd love something to eat. I haven't had anything since breakfast and it's almost three."

"No problem. Any preference for food?"

"A couple of slices of pizza and a diet Pepsi would be great."

"No problem," I said leaving the room.

Outside the door were two security guards. I turned to the two guards and said, "If he tries to leave, you are to call me and stop him from leaving."

"You got it." The taller guard promised.

I ordered two slices of pizza and a diet Pepsi for Dr. Edwards then I went in search of Mr. Roberts. I found him in another of the private rooms in the Emergency Room area. I walked into the room to find the Chief of Staff in the room reading over Mr. Roberts' chart. Mrs. Roberts was quietly sitting at her husband's bedside. She appeared to be in shock. I went over to her immediately.

"Mrs. Roberts?" I said softly. She looked up at me blankly.

"I'm Diana Goyeau from your husband's office," I said. "We met at the Holiday Party last year."

"Oh yes. Diana from Canada," she said with a smile.

"Is there anything that you need?" I asked.

"No, dear. I'm fine. My son is on his way to the hospital."

"Is there anyone else you need to get in touch with?" I asked

"No. There's just our son. You can have your press conference any time you need to."

"Thank you ma'am," I said.

I turned to the Chief of Staff, "Are you ready?" He nodded.

We walked out of the Mr. Roberts' room and went back to escort Dr. Edwards to the press conference. Just as I had suspected, he was trying to get past the two security guards.

"Really, Dr. Edwards, I didn't think you would really force me to play hardball," I said with a smile.

"Can't blame a man for trying. Are we ready for the show?" he asked.

"If you'll come with us, I'll try to make this as quick and painless as possible."

"That would be the first thing today that was quick and painless," he said with a taut smile.

Chapter Four

🜊

I couldn't believe my eyes when she walked into the room. She was breathtaking. I hadn't expected that. I didn't trust myself to not make a fool of myself. She was petite and slender with beautiful brown eyes. She had the most unbelievable red hair. Chelsea's hair was more brown than red. This woman's hair was carrot red, but it wasn't unflattering. It was striking.

Her name was Diana. I couldn't quite place her accent. It wasn't the traditional Boston accent I had finally adjusted to after living here since June. She was here to do damage control. I couldn't believe she had the gall to threaten me into staying for her press conference. And then she caught me trying to sneak out of the hospital. Fabulous.

We walked into the press conference together: Diana, The Chief of Staff and the Head of Emergency Surgery. I was not looking forward to this. Diana began the news conference.

"Ladies and Gentlemen," she addressed the crowd of reporters. She had a commanding voice for a petite woman, "If you would please take seats, we'll get this started. I know you all have deadlines coming up."

Surprisingly, they sat down and she began.

"Good Afternoon, My name is Diana Goyeau from the Public Relations office at UMASS General Hospital. I'll spell that for you, it's G-O-Y-E-A-U. I'm going to fill you in on the events of the accident and Dr. Cooper, our Chief of Staff, will brief you on the conditions of those involved and then you will have the opportunity to ask questions. With a little bit of patience you will have all the information you need."

I was impressed with her. She could not be more than thirty, yet she was commanding a room full of seasoned reporters.

"At approximately one this afternoon, Mr. Ezekiel Roberts and his wife were traveling down Washington Street in Boston when Mr. Roberts struck Dr. Steven Edwards, who is seated to my left. Dr. Edwards suffered a broken arm as a result. Mr. and Mrs. Roberts initially were unharmed in the accident, however, upon getting out of his car to inspect Dr. Edwards, Mr. Roberts called 911 then apparently suffered a heart attack. When Dr. Edwards regained consciousness, he helped to perform CPR on Mr. Roberts until paramedics arrived. Mr. Roberts and Dr. Edwards were both taken here for treatment. I will now have Dr. Cooper update you on the conditions of Dr. Edwards and Mr. Roberts."

"Thank you Diana," Dr. Cooper said as Diana stepped away from the podium and came to stand behind me.

"Mr. and Mrs. Roberts and Dr. Edwards were brought to the emergency room this afternoon. Mrs. Roberts' injuries were the least serious of the three. She was treated for minor injuries and remained with her husband. Dr. Edwards has a broken left arm. Mr. Roberts sustained the most serious injuries. While he was uninjured in the car accident, Mr. Roberts had a massive coronary on the scene. Dr. Edwards and a bystander began CPR until the paramedics arrived. When the paramedics arrived they were able to restart Mr. Roberts' heart, but unfortunately he had suffered a lack of oxygen to his brain, and consequently Mr. Roberts has slipped into a coma. His family is with him now."

Dr. Cooper left the podium. Diana stood again at the podium.

"Thank you Dr. Cooper. Ladies and Gentlemen, are there any questions?"

There were a few more questions about Mr. Roberts' prognosis. Dr. Cooper took those questions. There was one for me.

"Dr. Edwards?" I picked my head up and looked at the reporter.

"What were you doing in Boston?"

"I stopped to see a friend that was in town. I happened to be at the wrong place at the wrong time followed by the right place at the right time."

Diana intervened and ended the press conference. We walked out of the pressroom and into another private room. She turned to me and smiled. "Thank you Dr. Edwards," she said. "I know you want to get home. Did you drive into the city or take the train?"

"Actually, I took the train in."

"Let me be the first to offer you a ride home. I don't think the hospital would like you taking multiple trains home to your house in North Andover."

"Thanks, but I'd rather just get home. Like I said, it's been a really bad day."

"All the more reason, I must insist that you accept the hospital's offer for a ride home."

"If I can leave in the next five to ten minutes," I accepted. I never expected her to be able to do it. I assumed she was offering to call a car service. What I hadn't expected was her getting her own car and offering to drive me personally.

We were headed up to North Andover in less than ten minutes. I was surprised at her car. It was a Saab convertible. It was about three years old and very well maintained. I noticed that her back seat was filled with boxes.

"Moving?" I asked.

"Something like that," she said avoiding eye contact.

We continued to drive north on I 93. I was fighting the sleep of the medication and the soreness of my broken arm. I needed to stay awake to give her directions. I needed to talk or I would fall asleep. The easiest thing to do was to talk to Diana.

"So Ms. Goyeau, where are you from originally? I can't quite place your accent." I was concentrating on the road and her answer.

"I'm from Canada originally."

"A Canadian, eh?" I said with a smile.

She laughed, "I've stopped doing the "eh" thing. I've spent too much time in the US now. When I go home I pick it up again."

"How'd you end up in Boston?" I asked.

"Long story and lots of boxes," she said. "What about you? You're from New York?"

"How'd you guess that?"

"Your accent. It's definitely not Boston."

"Guilty as charged. I'm from New York City. I moved up here in June."

We were finally in North Andover. I had bought a new construction house on Salem Street and I had paid a fortune for it. My mom and dad had helped me out. They had sold their house in Bellerose, Long Island almost two years ago and put some of the money away for me each year. I had a nice down payment, but it was still tight every month. Between the malpractice insurance and the new office, I had quite a bit of money going out in bills. I knew I was going to be OK in the long run. I just needed to get past this first year. I had applied to teach a biology class this spring at Merrimack College in North Andover.

She pulled up in front of my house. "Nice house doc. I should have gone into medicine," she looked over at me and frowned, "Are you sure you're OK?"

I was beginning to feel the pain again. My arm was beginning to pound. I must have seemed a bit gray. I knew the drugs were wearing off. I needed to get another dose in me. I had the next dose of pain prescription with me.

I got out of the car and Diana surprised me by getting out and walking me to the front door. She walked in the door with me. I immediately went into the kitchen, grabbed a bottle of water from the refrigerator, and took the next set of painkillers and settled myself on the couch.

"Thanks for taking me all the way home. It really wasn't necessary." I said. I was getting more and more tired.

"Trust me it was necessary. I'm going to leave my card on your kitchen counter. If you need to get in touch with me, feel free to call."

"Thanks." I was beginning to feel the effects of the medicine.

Diana turned and left the house and I began to fall asleep on the couch. It was around five and I thought I could probably sleep until the next morning. I fell asleep. I heard the door open again. I tried to open my eyes. I could see a woman's figure in the living room.

"Chelsea?" I called out. She came over to me. She pushed the hair back from my forehead.

"Chelsea. I'm sorry," I said grabbing her hand and bringing it to my lips, "I didn't mean to tell him about the baby. I'm sorry."

"It's OK," she said. "Just go to sleep. You need to go to sleep"

"OK. I loved you Chelsea. I just wanted to make sure you were OK. I'm sorry."

I woke up around eleven that night. I was sore and my mind was fuzzy. I was trying to piece things together. I stumbled into the kitchen. I was surprised to see Diana Goyeau's card on my counter top. I popped another painkiller and headed upstairs. What an unbelievable day. I had to call my parents the next morning and tell them there was no way I was coming down for Thanksgiving. I wouldn't be able to drive the five to six hours to the eastern tip of Long Island with only one arm. I would also be better off staying away from Tommy for a while. I definitely needed to stay away from Chelsea.

I had dreamt that she was here at my house. I knew it wasn't real. I had taken her hand in mine at one point. I just hoped that I hadn't made a fool of myself in front of Diana. I had been so loaded up with drugs I couldn't trust myself to not make a fool of myself. That would've been twice in one day that I made a fool of myself.

Sunday came and I headed out to church on the Merrimack College campus where I had put in an application to teach a class in the spring. I hoped to boost my income by teaching class one night a week. The college campus was beautiful in the fall and mass was quick. I returned to my house and called my parents' home.

"Hi Mom," I said to my mother when she answered the phone.

"Hello Steven," My mom said. "When are you coming down for Thanksgiving?"

"Actually that's why I'm calling. I can't make it down. I'm sorry to cancel last minute but I have an excuse."

"This had better be good," she said with a laugh.

"I broke my left arm yesterday. I was hit by a car in Boston and broke my left arm."

"You're joking. Right?" I could hear the shock in her voice.

"No, unfortunately, I'm not. I can't drive all the way to Long Island with only one arm. I should be fine for Christmas and I promise I will be there."

"Let me get your father on the phone," she said. I heard her call my father. "Kevin, come here. Steven's on the phone."

My father was a retired eye doctor. It was not something I had wanted to go into. I preferred working with children and specialized in pediatrics. Despite the fact that he was an eye doctor, he thought he knew everything.

"Hello Steven," my father said. "What's new?"

"I broke my arm yesterday."

"Tell him how!" my mother was saying in the background.

"I was hit by a car in Boston," I said.

"Where did they take you?"

"The driver was the head of Public Relations for UMASS General, so they took me there. The driver actually suffered a massive coronary and does not have a good prognosis."

"You were very lucky," my father said. "You rest. I know you Steven. You're going to try to over do it."

"Now you sound like mom," I chuckled. "Actually I'm going to spend some time at the hospital this weekend with one of my patients. He needs a few tests and I think he and his parents will be more comfortable with me there."

"That's very nice of you dear. We'll call you again this weekend to make sure everything is OK," I heard my mother say from the background.

I turned on the TV and shuffled through the channels until I reached the football games. It was half time of the first round of games. Instead of a having a roundup of scores a local news bulletin came on the television.

"We're going live to UMASS General for an update on Director of Public Relations Ezekiel Roberts."

There she was again, Diana Goyeau. She was about to begin the press conference.

"Good afternoon ladies and gentlemen. At ten this morning, Mrs. Roberts decided to remove her husband, Ezekiel, from life support. Shortly afterward, he was pronounced dead. As Mr.

Roberts had decided to donate his organs, they were harvested and have benefited five other people. The hospital would like to take this opportunity to thank Mrs. Roberts for her courageous decision. Mr. Roberts, as you know, served this hospital as head of Public Relations for the last thirty years. He will be greatly missed. Funeral arrangements for Mr. Roberts are being handled by his family. The hospital will hold a memorial service a week from Monday. Thank you."

Crap. I thought. I found her business card on the counter and dialed the number. Her voicemail picked up. I waited for her greeting to be over. I was shocked that her greeting was in English, French and Spanish.

"Hi. Ms. Goyeau. It's Dr. Steven Edwards. I just saw your press conference on TV. I was calling to see if you would share with me the arrangements for Mr. Roberts. I would like to send flowers and pay my respects to his family. Please call me back at my house."

The football game had come back on the screen and I settled in to watch the Patriots play. I very rarely saw the NY teams play. The exception to this rule would be when the Patriots and Jets played each other. A tight rivalry in the last few years, it was great to watch. My arm was less painful today. I thought I would be able to get through office hours tomorrow. Mondays were always terrible in the morning. Every parent whose child became ill over the weekend came in with his or her child. It was always a busy morning. I had planned to go down to UMASS Monday evening to see Zachary Young. Zach was checking in on Monday morning for the battery of tests that I had ordered for him. By Monday afternoon, he was sure to know the outcome of those tests. I thought it might make it easier for him to see a familiar face.

Chapter Five

♥

I left Dr. Edwards' house a little puzzled. I had forgotten my car keys on his counter and I had to go back into the house to get them. I had knocked, but he hadn't answered. The door was unlocked and I quickly walked into the house. He had called out a woman's name when I walked in. I went over to the couch.

I couldn't resist pushing the hair off his forehead. His eyes were glazed over from the pain and the drugs.

"Chelsea, I'm sorry," he said grabbing my hand and bringing it to his lips. "I didn't mean to tell him about the baby. I'm sorry."

He was so worried. I could tell from his face that he was sorry. He was so sad. I knew he needed comfort.

"It's OK," I whispered. "Just go to sleep. You need to go to sleep"

"OK. I loved you Chelsea. I just wanted to make sure you were OK. I'm sorry."

I walked out the door and sat behind the wheel of my car. Whoever this woman Chelsea was I had the feeling something had gone terribly wrong. I was driving back toward my apartment in Cambridge when my cell phone went off again. It was the hospital again.

"Diana?" It was Dr. Cooper.

"Yes Dr. Cooper?" I said. I needed to impress him if I wanted to take Mr. Roberts' job.

"Mr. Roberts family has decided to take him off life support. I need you back at the hospital for the next round of press conferences."

"No problem. I just left Dr. Edwards at his house," I informed him. I was only a block from my apartment so I grabbed a few things and put them in a bag. I was sure it was going to be a long day, if not night, at the hospital.

I walked into my office and put down my bag of things. I called Dr. Cooper's office immediately to let him know I was back in the building. I camped out in my office waiting for the next call from Dr. Cooper. I was surprised by the fact that I was handling all the press conferences. I knew I was on call this weekend, but I was the least senior of the three public relations officers. I remembered Terrence was going out of town the whole week because I had picked up Thanksgiving weekend from him. Being Canadian, Thanksgiving weekend wasn't as big of a deal to me. I was glad to see something occupy my time. It would help to keep my mind off the trip I was supposed to take back to Chicago with Patrick. Michelle, the other public relations officer was a real viper, I was surprised she hadn't shown up at the office since the whole incident started. I guessed that she was away this weekend as well. If you were out of town, the story of Mr. Ezekiel Roberts wouldn't make the news. The only reason it made the news in Boston was due to his high profile in the charity circuit.

Truth be known, Ezekiel Roberts was the reason I had the job at UMASS General. He was working with the Special Olympics last year while I had been doing public relations work for them. I loved working for the Special Olympics, but I learned very fast that there was no money in non-profit work. He had been impressed with a fundraiser that I had coordinated for them. Before I knew it, he had called me to fill an opening in his staff. I was very grateful for the opportunity to work at the hospital. The events of the day were upsetting on a personal level for me. Mr. Roberts had always been very helpful as well as supportive.

My office phone rang. I grabbed it on the first ring.

"Diana Goyeau," I answered.

"Diana, it's Dr. Cooper. I'm upstairs with Mrs. Roberts. She was asking for you."

"What room number?"

"Room 525," he said without a second of hesitation.

"I'm on my way," I said hanging up the phone. I checked my appearance in the mirror on the back of my door. I was a little mussed but I was presentable. It was close to eight at night.

I knocked softly on the door.

"Come in," came the reply.

"Mrs. Roberts," I said addressing her, "you wanted to see me?"

I knelt down next to the chair where she was seated beside her husband's bed. His chest was rising and falling with the movement of the ventilator. The beeps of the various machines were keeping time.

"Yes dear," Mrs. Roberts turned to me. She was around sixty years old but had never quite looked her age. Today's events seemed to add to her age.

"What can I do for you Mrs. Roberts?" I asked gently.

"Not a thing dear. I just wanted to go over some things with you. I know Ezekiel is not going to improve. He had a living will that stipulated what should be done if something like this happened. My son went home to get it out of our safe. I need to produce it in order to start the process."

I nodded my head. This must be a terrible decision for her to have to make.

"Mr. Roberts always liked you. I'm glad that you were one this weekend and not Terrence or Michelle."

"Thank you Mrs. Roberts."

"Please call me Emily."

"Fine. Emily it is. What do you need to go over with me?" I asked.

"I want to spend tonight with Ezekiel. Tomorrow morning, my son, his wife and their children will come to the hospital. After we have had a chance to say good-bye..."

"I understand." I said to her.

"We would like to keep the funeral as private as possible. I will have a list and invitations for you on Monday. Could you see that they get to the appropriate people?"

Again I nodded, "The hospital, I'm sure, will arrange a memorial service. Is there a day that is preferable to you?"

"A week from tomorrow would be fine. I will leave that up to you and Dr. Cooper. Thank you for that."

"Is there anything else I can get you? Have you eaten dinner?"

"You know, I haven't eaten since lunch. Is there a restaurant close by that could send a dinner?"

"No problem. Do you have a preference for the type of food?"

"Seafood would be wonderful. How about salmon? Mr. Roberts loved salmon and good bottle of white wine."

"No problem." I turned to leave the room. Dr. Cooper had been standing at the door. Instead of entering the room, he followed me into the hallway.

"Thank you Diana," he said. "I'm not really sure if she's aware of everything right now. Call Harvard Gardens and arrange the dinner she wants. Tell them it's for the hospital. We have an account with them."

I nodded.

"I hope you didn't have big plans for this weekend or for this week for that matter."

"No sir. I had nothing really planned for the next week. I was already on for Thanksgiving weekend anyway."

"Go order that food and get some rest, but I wouldn't wander too far. Even though we don't anticipate anything new before the morning, you never know."

Again I nodded.

"Did Dr. Edwards make it home all right?"

"I left him at his house. He was settling himself in on the couch before I left."

"I really hope this doesn't blow up in our face."

"I'm sure it won't."

I called Harvard Gardens from my office phone. I ordered Mrs. Roberts' salmon dinner and her bottle of wine. They were very cordial on the phone and put it on the hospital's account. I then ordered take out for myself from Shangri-La, the Chinese restaurant around the corner. When Mrs. Roberts' dinner arrived, I personally brought it up to her. She thanked me and I returned to my office. I settled myself behind my desk and began to check my e-mail.

Before I knew it, the clock on my wall read midnight. I went upstairs to check on Mrs. Roberts again. She was asleep in the chair by her husband's side. The bottle of wine was half gone. I went to the nurses' station and asked if there were an empty room someplace that I could crash. They took pity on me and showed me to a private room at the end of the hall. I shut off the lights, curled up on the bed, and began to prepare myself for the events of the following day. I fell asleep before I could even think of a good plan.

Chapter Six

❦

I had somehow made it through the day on Monday. At around three, my partners had pity on me and sent me on my way. I should have gone home and rested but I was anxious about Zachary. I made my way to the commuter rail line and arrived in Boston as the evening rush to leave was beginning. I was protective of my left arm, which was still a little sore. I had to cut a dress shirt to fit over my cast. I went without my suit coat and tie. I had tried to tie my tie but couldn't quite do it with one hand. When I arrived at the office, the nurses laughed and told me to not bother with the tie.

I arrived at MASS General and asked for Zachary's room. He was in the pediatric ward and had yet to be transferred. I made my way upstairs and asked for directions at the nurses' station. I finally found myself outside his room.

His mother was sleeping in the chair by his bed. I walked in and Zachary saw me. I held my fingers to my lips and pointed at his mom. He had an IV in his left arm. Quietly, I helped him move off the bed with the IV pole. He was moving gingerly. I knew they had done a bone marrow aspiration on him today. He was ten but a very tall boy for his age. His hospital room was next to the patient lounge and we made our way in there.

I had grabbed his bed pillow for him and put it on the chair. He had loose fitting sweatpants on under his hospital gown. He sat on the pillowed chair and smiled at me.

"What happened to your arm?" he asked.

"Long story. What's up with you?"

"Leukemia. You knew didn't you?" Zachary questioned.

I nodded, "I did too much work at NYU to not know. That's why I ordered the tests for today. How are your mom and dad?"

"My mom's crying a lot. My dad left at twelve after the doctor told them. He went to tell them at work that he's taking the rest of the week off."

I nodded, "What exactly did they tell you about what you have?"

"They didn't tell me much. They left some stuff for my parents to read." He said.

"I'll go grab the papers. I'm sure there's a video game cart. Maybe I can find that too. You're sure to beat me. I only have one working arm." He laughed as I got up.

I walked out into the hallway and went to the nurses' station. I introduced myself to them and asked if they had a video game cart.

"Sure," said the nurse behind the desk. She left to get the key to the closet. I quietly went into Zach's room. His mother was still sleeping. I grabbed the material on the bedside table. I walked back into the hall to see Diana Goyeau standing there.

"Ms. Goyeau!" I called to her.

She turned and smiled, "Dr. Edwards. How is your arm?"

"Sore, but better than yesterday," I said. She was dressed in a short gray skirt with a white blouse. Her red hair was pulled away from her face in a twist. She was really very beautiful.

"What brings you back to Mass General?" she asked.

"I actually have a patient that was here today for tests. I came to see him and his parents."

"Who's your patient?" she asked. I was looking down at her. I was just over six feet tall but she was rather tiny.

"Zachary Young," I answered.

"That's actually who I came up to see. He was just diagnosed with leukemia."

"He's in the lounge waiting for me and the video game cart. His mom's asleep in his room."

The nurse came back with the video game cart. "Hey Diana. I'm surprised you have a minute to spare."

"It's about all I have the next week, but thanks for calling me," she said. She took the cart and began pushing it toward the lounge. I began walking with her toward the lounge.

"I left you a voicemail yesterday afternoon," I said. "I was sorry to hear about Mr. Roberts."

"It was a crazy day yesterday. I left you a message at home. I guess you didn't get it."

"No. I came from the office straight here. My partners felt sorry for me and sent me home early. I knew what Zachary was up against so I came here instead of going home."

"That was nice of you. I'm a liaison with the Leukemia and Lymphoma Society. When there is a new diagnosis in the hospital, the nurses call me. I stop up and introduce myself to the patient and the family."

We were at the door to the lounge. Zachary Young was sitting in a chair watching TV fiddling with his IV pole.

"Zach," I called to him. He turned to look at me, "Look what I found."

"The girl or the cart?" He joked

"They're both pretty impressive," I said smiling. "I mean the video game cart."

Diana pushed it into the room and introduced herself.

"Hi. I'm Diana. You must be Zachary," she smiled. I thought that if I were greeted with that smile, I'd forget any video game.

"Zach is fine," he said in the third person.

"I work in the hospital but I also work for the Leukemia and Lymphoma Society," she explained. She took out her business card and gave it to him.

"Your last name is really funny. How do you say it?" Zach asked.

She laughed, "It's French. You say it Goy-O. I get that a lot here. It wasn't such a problem in Canada." She plugged in the cart and was setting up the games.

"What do you want to play?" she asked. "They have Madden Football."

"That sounds good," Zach said. "Are you going to play doc?"

"Why don't you play Ms. Goyeau? I don't think I'd be much of a challenge with one arm," I said laughing. Diana turned and smiled at me.

"Please call me Diana."

She began playing Madden Football with him. She was good. I assumed she wouldn't be as good as she was. She seemed more of a girlie girl. Before the first half was over, she was winning. Zach was not too thrilled to be losing, let alone losing to a girl.

"Why don't we play tag team? Dr. Edwards, do you want to take over?" she said to me. I smiled and took over the controls.

"Zach I'm going to go down and introduce myself to your mom." Diana walked out and Zach and I continued to play the game.

"Doc?" Zach said to me, "I want to know as much about this as possible. I need to know. I'm not a baby. I can understand. Can I count on you helping me get the information I need?"

I looked at him. "You got it. Do you have an e-mail account?"

"No, we don't have a computer at home."

"You don't need a computer to have an e-mail." I turned and looked around until I saw what I was looking for; in the lounge there was a computer. "There's a computer here that you can use."

I put the controls to the game down and I walked over to the computer. I connected to the Internet and went to Google. I set up a gmail account for him. I had the necessary information sent in a text message to my phone. I activated the account and added him to my address book.

"Listen," I said to him, "I don't want you surfing the web looking for things. Some of the things you will read will scare you. I'm going to look at your chart before I go and I will start researching and let you know what I find. Do we have a deal?" I held out my hand to him.

He shook it.

"Let's go see your mom," I suggested. I helped him get up with his IV pole and pillow. We made our way back to his room where Diana was sitting with Zach's mom.

"Hi Mrs. Young," I said at the door.

"Dr. Edwards. What happened to your arm?" she asked as she got up to help Zach with his pole.

"I broke it on Saturday," I said smiling at Diana.

"You should be home resting," she said to me as though se were my mother.

"I wanted to see how things went," I said.

"They could have gone better. Jeff will be sad that he missed you," she said. "I'll tell him you stopped by."

Zach sat down heavily on his bed. I noticed how tired he looked. I hated to leave, but I knew they needed time together as a family.

"I've got to head out, but I'll stop by again later this week. Zach keep using that computer in the lounge," I offered my hand for a five. He gave me five and I gave his mother a hug. I walked out of his room. Diana followed me. It was almost six.

"Ms. Goyeau, " I said to her, "thanks for stopping in to see them. They're going to need a lot of support during this process."

"No problem," she said grinning up at me.

"Do you have plans for dinner?" I asked.

"Probably take out on the way home," she said. "It's going to be a busy week for me."

"Could I persuade you to go to dinner with me?" I said. "I owe you for that ride home on Saturday. I don't remember much of it."

"You were a little out of it," she said with a smile. "Dinner would be nice. I'm warning you though. I need to keep my cell on. I usually don't do that, but it's a busy a week and we're short staffed."

"No explanations necessary. Especially since I was the cause of your really busy week."

We walked out of the hospital. It was November but the weather in Boston was unseasonably warm.

"Do you mind a little walk?" she asked.

"No. I broke my arm, not my leg," I quipped with a laugh.

She laughed at my joke and explained, "There's a really great restaurant on Bowdin. The Red Hat Restaurant."

"I've heard of it, but I've never been there." I told her.

We walked down Cambridge Street to Bowdin Street. We arrived at the Red Hat Restaurant. There was about a ten-minute wait so we sat near the bar.

"Do you want a drink?" I asked.

"Just a Coke. I'm pretty much on call this whole week," She said.

I ordered her a Coke and a Sam Adams for me. "I probably shouldn't have a beer, but I need a drink after seeing Zach and his mom."

"That's got to be one of the worst things to have to do as a doctor," she said turning the ice in her Coke. "Especially being a pediatrician. Telling someone they have a life threatening disease is bad enough but explaining it to a kid has to be the worst."

"I tried to prepare his parents on Friday that I thought this was a distinct possibility. Zach's parents chose to shield him from it, but Zach doesn't want to be left out of the loop so I set him up with an e-mail account. I'm going to send him information that he'll understand," I paused to take a drink.

"I hate getting the call from pediatrics that there is a new case of leukemia on the floor. Depending on the type, it can be devastating."

"I'm going to have to learn more about the types. I know a little about the disease but not as much as Zach will want to know."

"I have some stuff I can send you," she volunteered.

"So let me get this straight. You work for Mass General but you also work for the Leukemia and Lymphoma Society."

"Kind of. I've always done work with the Leukemia Society so when I took the job at Mass General, it made sense to continue it. I really just pass along information to the patients."

"You wouldn't work for them full time?" I asked.

"I don't mean to sound money hungry, but there's not enough money in non-profit work. I tried that route when I first came to Boston. I practically ended up homeless," She said with a laugh. I thought about the boxes in the backseat of her car.

Our table was ready and we moved into the dining area. We sat down with our menus and looked everything over. Since I had never been there before, I asked for her opinion.

"Almost anything is good off the menu. What are you in the mood for?"

"I'd love to get the ribs, but I don't want to make a complete fool of myself yet again in front of you," I said with a smile. "I think I'll settle for the baked scallops. If I ordered an appetizer, would you help me eat it?"

"Most definitely. I didn't get a chance to eat lunch, so I'm actually starved."

"How about the potato skins?" I asked.

"They're great," she smiled back. We ordered when the waitress came over. I switched over to diet Pepsi after I finishing my one beer.

"What did you mean you were the cause of my bad week?" she asked.

"The car accident was my fault. I had a really bad conversation with someone and wasn't paying attention to anything. I didn't even see Mr. Roberts nor did I hear the car horn."

"Was the conversation with Chelsea?" she asked.

I was surprised she had guessed that. "Did I say something Saturday when I was all drugged up?"

"Kind of. I had gotten out to my car when I realized I left my keys on your kitchen counter. I knocked, but you didn't answer. I walked in and you called her name. I walked over to you on the couch and you were apologizing for telling somebody about the baby."

I cringed. "Sorry about that. Chelsea is my best friend's sister. She was in town on Saturday. Her brother asked me to check up on her. He's not too sure about her new boyfriend. I checked up on her and the boyfriend irritated me. I said things I shouldn't have said. It's hard not to believe in instant karma when I was hit down the block from the scene of my bad judgment.

"Sorry," she said.

The waitress arrived with the potato skins. It was then that I realized cutting with one hand was also going to be a problem. She laughed and had pity on me.

"My brother Sam broke his arm when he was in high school. I ended up cutting most of his dinners for him. It sucks. In about two weeks you'll be able to do more but then the itching will start. Before you know it you'll be sticking anything and everything into your cast to scratch that itch."

"Thanks for the tip," I said. "Why didn't you become a doctor?"

"I thought about it for a while. But I was never really good with the site of blood."

I laughed. "So how does a Canadian end up this side of the border?"

"My parents live just over the border in Canada. My dad actually worked in Detroit his whole adult life. My parents used to go over the border with the three of us to shop. They used to dress me in layers of clothes to get the stuff back in without paying the taxes. One day I almost gave them up. After that they made sure that I was tire and almost asleep before crossing the border."

I started laughing at the image she put in my mind. I could almost see this little red headed chatterbox volunteering all the information the border patrol needed.

"I actually went to college at University of Notre Dame and then did my masters at DePaul. After finishing at DePaul, I had the opportunity to move to Boston. I opted to take it. Finding a job out here was an adventure."

"How's that?" I asked. The waitress came to clear the empty plates.

"When you apply for a job as a Canadian, you need to have a specific area of expertise. Since my original visa was to go to school for public relations, I had to get a job in public relations. Not the easiest thing in the Boston area. It took several tries before I was offered my job at Mass General. It was Mr. Roberts that actually offered me my job about a year ago. He stole me away from Special Olympics."

"Wow. I didn't realize there would be so many problems getting a job," I said. "I guess I'm spoiled. I could have taken over my father's practice if I had become an optometrist, but I really like working with kids. My dad's roommate from college was getting ready to retire and offered me his share of a practice in Lawrence. I bought in."

"Lawrence. That's a rough town," she said. Our dinners had arrived and she cut up my food for me. I was embarrassed that she had to help me again.

"Thanks," I said. "I like it. I wanted to make a difference but still make a living."

"Now you sound like me," she said with a laugh.

"Are you handling Mr. Roberts' funeral and memorial service?" I asked.

"Pretty much," she said looking down at her food. She had ordered a panini. "I called your house this morning. Mr. Roberts will be buried on Wednesday. His funeral is by invitation only. All the invitations were sent out today. There's a public memorial service a week from today at the hospital."

"Could I get Mrs. Roberts' home address to send her my condolences?"

"That I can do." She took out a paper from her purse and wrote down the address for me.

"Thanks," I said taking the paper from her. I folded it and put it in my shirt pocket. We had finished our dinner, and I motioned for the waitress to bring me the check. I checked my watch; it was after eight. "I should get going. Thank you for dinner. I'm sure I'll run into you at the hospital while visiting Zach."

"Thank you for dinner. It's been a while since I actually sat down and ate dinner with someone else."

I laughed, "I find that hard to believe."

"No, really. It really has been a while between work and life in general. I've been eating way too much take-out." She seemed to stiffen after her last statement. "I really should let you go, you have a much longer ride home than I do."

She hurriedly got up from the table looking at the bar area behind me. I stood with her and glanced behind me to see what had gotten her so flustered. A group of men had come into the bar area and were ordering drinks at the bar. One of them nudged another and nodded in our direction. I saw a tall brown haired man turn around and smile. He lifted a glass to Diana. She smiled politely and we began walking out of the restaurant.

"Sorry about that," she said to me as we walked out the restaurant door. We began walking back toward the hospital.

"Friends of yours?" I asked.

"Sort of," she answered. She seemed a little tense about the situation.

"Do you celebrate Thanksgiving?" I asked changing the topic of conversation.

"Technically, yes," she said with a laugh. "Thanksgiving Day in Canada is actually Columbus Day Weekend in the US but since we lived so close to the border, we used to celebrate it again in November."

"What about this year?" I asked.

"I'm on call at the hospital all weekend long," she said. "What about you? Are you headed home to New York?"

"I was originally going to go to New York, but I can't drive that long with only one hand. It would be an accident waiting to happen. If Zach is still in the hospital, I was planning to stop in to see him and his family."

"That sounds like fun. I know the staff that works that day has a Thanksgiving dinner. What if I put together something with them on pediatrics?" she was smiling.

I was stunned at how much her smile added to her face. "That would be great. Please let me know what I need to bring." I took out my business card and gave it to her.

"No problem," she said. "I'll see you on Thursday then." We were standing in front of the hospital entrance.

"I'm looking forward to it," I said and she turned to walk away.

"Diana," I called out to her. She turned around. "Don't let the sort of stuff bother you. It's not worth it."

She laughed, "Don't I know that, but thanks for the tip!"

I stood there watching her walk away. The guy with the glass of scotch had unsettled her. That amazed me. She had been so calm at both press conferences but yet this one man walking into the bar and raising his glass to her had had the ability to set her on edge. Suddenly Thanksgiving was actually looking pretty good. I turned and made my way toward North Station where I would catch the commuter rail to North Andover.

Chapter Seven

♥

I had walked all the way to my office before I was able to control my racing heart. I hadn't seen Patrick in almost a month. It really set me off. I had moved out of the townhouse at the beginning of November. I had actually slept on the floor at my friend Cindy's apartment. It was in the beginning of November when I was packing up things that I had found pictures of Patrick and another woman. It was then that I decided to move out completely. I returned to the townhouse only when I knew Patrick wouldn't be there.

Yet, there he was with all his friends from work. I knew that would eventually happen. He worked in the financial center. It was only a matter of time before I crossed paths with him. I just wasn't prepared for it. I had really wanted to be prepared and to be at a better place emotionally. He seemed so smug with the glass of scotch in his hand toasting me. I wasn't sure what that was all about but I didn't want to find out.

What had Steven said, "Don't let that sort of stuff bother you. It's not worth it" made me smile. He had a really great outlook on life. And he wasn't bad to look at. I smiled again. I wouldn't mind seeing him again Thursday.

I walked into the apartment happy to be home. I had spent Saturday night at the hospital only to have to work late Sunday night. I arrived home last night at midnight and was back at work by eight on Monday morning. What fun Monday morning had been!

At nine, Michelle Dupree showed up at work. I had already been busy with the invitations for Mrs. Roberts. There were over three hundred people to invite to the funeral. I needed to send out the invitations by ten. Most of the people lived in the area but some were out-of-town. The area residents were being hand-delivered by a courier service while the out-of-town invitations needed to be at he post office by ten for express mail delivery. Michelle stopped into my office to be nasty to me.

"Well didn't you just land in it this weekend?" she said to me from the doorway to my office.

"Hi Michelle. How was your weekend?"

"Fine. I arrived home last night from Florida to find out that you had hogged the spotlight all weekend long." she complained.

"I was on call. You and Terrance were away. It's not like I enjoyed the events of the weekend. Mr. Roberts was a very kind man," I said.

"Whatever," she spat walking out of my doorway and heading down to her office.

Following Steven's advice and not letting her negative attitude get to me, I put my head back down and finished the out of town invites then took them personally to the post office. After the much needed fresh air, I finished the in-town guest list and had the courier service pick them from my office. I was about to go for lunch when I was called downstairs to the ER for another high profile patient.

I walked into the ER to discover a federal agent had been wounded in a raid. I found myself going in front of the cameras again to speak about his treatment. I knew Michelle would be green with envy. By the time I arrived in my office, I had three messages. The first was from Mrs. Roberts thanking me for the invitation work; many of her in town friends had already received them. The second message was from my mom who was just checking in. The third message was the one that broke my heart but at the same time had brought me into contact with Steven.

The third message was from the nurses in pediatrics. They were calling to tell me about a new leukemia patient in the hospital. I sat for a minute holding my head in my hands. It always made me sad to hear of a child being diagnosed with cancer. I made my way up to pediatrics at around five. That's when I saw Dr. Steve Edwards again.

I hadn't forgotten how good-looking he was. He was just over six feet tall but in comparison to my five foot four inches, he seemed gigantic. He was holding his coat with his arm that was in the cast they had put on him Saturday afternoon. I remembered he was a pediatrician but I was surprised to see him on the Pediatrics wing. He wasn't affiliated with the hospital.

I was shocked to find out that he was there to see the same patient I was: Zachary Young. Zachary had been the young boy diagnosed with leukemia that morning. He was the last thing I had to do before my very long day was over. I met with him briefly and with his mother. I was surprised at how adult he seemed. I was surprised a second time when Dr. Edwards asked me to go to dinner with him. All I could think of was how terrible I looked. It had been a long last few days and I was sure my eyes showed the lack of sleep and my clothes were less than perfect.

Dinner was surprisingly pleasant. Usually doctors had stuffy personalities. Steven really wasn't your traditional doctor. He laughed at himself easily and made me laugh. It had been such a long time since I had laughed. The whole breakup with Patrick had taken its toll on me. In a bizarre twist of fate, dinner was winding down when I saw Patrick come into the bar area. I couldn't believe the really bad luck. I thought I had been smooth about wanting to leave, but Steven had noticed. By the time I was back at my office, I was more under control, but I was still unnerved.

"Don't let that sort of stuff bother you," was what he had said.

My cell phone rang. It was Cindy.

"What's up?" I said.

"You tell me *Miss TV press conference lady.*" She said with a laugh.

"I've been busy. What can I say?" I answered.

"How much running have you been doing lately?" she asked.

"Not as much as I should have. I need to get a good run in. I missed Sunday and today."

"Why did you miss today? I thought you were going to go for a run after work."

"I went out to dinner instead," I said. "With a hot doctor."

"I'd skip the run too. Who's the hot doctor?" she asked.

"It really wasn't like that. I just wanted to give you some hope. He's the doctor that Mr. Roberts hit with his car. He was at the hospital today checking up on one of his patients."

"Doctor Ken Doll," she said excitedly. "You went out to dinner with Dr. Ken Doll!"

"Yes, but you will never guess who strolled into the restaurant as we were getting ready to leave."

She groaned, "How did that go?"

"I smiled and left. I just finished calming down," I said. "By the way, I'm having Thanksgiving Dinner at the hospital with Dr. Ken Doll."

"No shit!" she gasped. "I'm almost sad I'm going to Hartford for Thanksgiving."

"I'll call you. I'm going to hit the gym tomorrow morning for a long run on the treadmill. I'm setting my alarm now." I was already lying in bed in my pajamas.

"How many miles are you up to now?" she asked. Cindy and I were planning to run the Boston Marathon this spring as part of the Team in Training program for the Leukemia and Lymphoma Society.

"I'm up to twelve miles. I'm racing in the ten mile Turkey Day run on Thanksgiving. I just hope the two days off is not going to kill me on Thursday."

"You have everything out of Patrick's townhouse?"

"Last box filled on Saturday right before Dr. Ken Doll was hit." I said.

"Focus on that right now. You're going to the funeral on Wednesday right?" she asked.

"Yes." I wasn't looking forward to that.

"Any shot at getting Roberts' job?" Cindy asked.

"Maybe," I answered. I could hope for that. I was doing the job right now but not getting the pay for it. I honestly hoped I would be offered his job.

"I'll have my dad pray for you," Cindy said. "Go get some sleep. You looked tired this afternoon."

"I am tired," I said. "And thank your dad for the prayers.

I hung up the phone, turned out the lights and was asleep before I knew it.

Chapter Eight

♼

I never thought a broken arm could cause so many problems in daily life. I was very limited in what I could get done at work. I thanked God every day it wasn't my right arm. That would have made my life impossible. At least with a broken left arm, I could still write and complete most of the work I needed to do at the office. Tuesday at the office went better than Monday and Wednesday was better than Tuesday. I had no office hours on Friday because had planned to be in Long Island. After work I would spend hours on line looking for information for Zach on his particular type of leukemia.

Zach had the most common of childhood leukemia: Acute Lymphocatic Leukemia. This was also the most curable form of leukemia. The key was treating it in time. The acute part of the disease meant that the leukemia was fast moving. It needed aggressive treatment through chemotherapy and a bone marrow transplant. The Lymphocatic meant the leukemia was found in his lymph system. I was hopeful that the doctors would easily put him in remission. I made notes about the online information and explained it to Zach via e-mail.

Diana Goyeau had been an interesting element to the equation. She had sent me a few things via e-mail that were informative. She had been very helpful in providing information that would help him understand the disease with which he had been diagnosed. I knew the work that she was doing for Zachary wasn't part of her job in public relations at Mass General. I wondered why she was so passionate about working with the Leukemia and Lymphoma Society. It was a question I planned to ask her on Thanksgiving Day.

Thanksgiving Day. At first I hadn't been looking forward to spending Thanksgiving in Boston but with Diana there as well it was becoming more appealing. My mother was always worried about me not eating enough. She had ordered me a pie from a gourmet pie company that delivered. Wednesday morning, the Dutch Apple pie arrived at my office. It had been frozen for delivery. I immediately put in the freezer and e-mailed Diana to let her know I had apple pie. I also asked if there was anything else that I needed to bring.

The staff had taken care of everything with each person on that day bringing a side dish. They had ordered a turkey from a local restaurant. I ordered a second turkey from a Boston Market near Mass General. With my broken arm, I really couldn't carry much else. I wentto the local bookstore and picked up a few books for Zachary to take his mind off his disease.

I packed everything into a shopping bag and headed into Boston at around eleven on Thanksgiving morning. I arrived at Boston Market added the additional turkey to the load I was carrying. I had purchased a new laptop case with a shoulder strap. I had my laptop with me in order to help Zachary find more information about his disease. He was slated to start chemotherapy on Friday. This made the meal more like a last supper than a meal of thanks. Both his parents were going to be at the hospital today as well as his older brother and younger sister who were going to be tested for a potential bone marrow match on Friday morning. Friday morning, Zach would be permanently moved to the pediatric cancer wing.

After checking in at the front desk, I made my way up to the pediatrics floor. I stopped at the nurses' station and introduced myself.

"We were expecting you a little later," the head nurse said. 'The turkey we ordered won't be here for another two hours."

"No problem. I didn't have anything else to do today." I said. "Here is another turkey breast and a pie my mom ordered. It should be defrosted by now."

One of the other nurses came and took the bag into the patient lounge where we would all be eating.

"Is Diana Goyeau here yet?" I asked.

"No. She'll probably be up in the next hour. She had a road race this morning and should be up from downstairs shortly."

I turned and walked into Zach's room puzzled by Diana. A road race on Thanksgiving Day? I had never heard of that, nor had I expected her to do something like that. Zachary, his older brother and his father were sitting in his room watching TV when I walked in. They were both happy to see me. Zach's mom and sister were taking a walk in the hospital. I settled into watching sports with them. There was a certain amount of male bonding that went on with watching sports. We were engrossed in the game when Diana walked in with Zach's mom and sister.

"Hey boys!" she said. "How's the game?"

I looked up and was stunned by the sight of her. She had on a pair of jeans with a brown sweater. It made her hair even more noticeable as well as all the more beautiful. She had a bright smile for Zachary and his family.

"What's up doc?" she asked with a smile. "How's the arm?"

"I'm not ready for the hospital football game, but I'm doing better than Monday," I said with a smile.

At half time, we moved into the lounge and ate with the other patients and the staff. The staff ate in shifts so as to monitor those children who needed more constant attention. We were sitting around the table after eating a very delicious Thanksgiving dinner when I asked Diana about her race.

"What road race did you run this morning?"

"The Thanksgiving Day race in Cambridge. Who told you about my road race?" she asked, a surprised look on her face.

"One of the nurses said that you had run a race this morning and were coming in after the race."

"I ran the 10-mile this morning. I'm training for the Boston Marathon this spring."

"Ten miles!" Zachary commented. "All at once?"

She laughed, "Yes. The marathon is longer. It's twenty-six point two miles. I've heard it's the point two that gets most people."

"What made you do that?" I inquired.

"Cindy, a friend of mine, talked me into it. I'm doing it with Team in Training."

"What's Team in Training?" Zachary piped in.

"It's a group of people that run and walk marathons all over the country, the world actually, to raise money for the Leukemia and Lymphoma Society."

"Have you ever done it before?"

"Nope. Today was the longest race I've ever run. I run about 12 miles a day right now. I'm hoping to finish the race. I'm not looking for a great time."

"That's so cool." Zach said.

I nodded. "I don't think I would be able to do that. I like to run but not 26 miles at once."

"I didn't think I'd be able to do it either but I've had a lot of support from the other runners and from my friends and family. I have my own website where people can donate money and where I can log my training hours." She was animated in telling us all about it. She obviously had a passion for her goal.

She looked at her watch. It was almost six. "I had better let Zachary get some rest. They're transferring him over tomorrow morning and beginning his treatment."

Zachary had a worried look on his face. She got up from the table and rubbed the top of his head. "Don't worry. Do you still have my business card?"

Zach nodded.

"My cell phone number is on there. Call me anytime you want to talk."

He nodded again and smiled up at her. I stood to leave as well.

Zachary's mom and dad stood up to say good-bye to both of us. Mrs. Young embraced both Diana and me. Mr. Young also hugged us both. They thanked us for spending our holiday with them. We walked down the hallway together toward the elevator. When we arrived at the elevator, Diana smiled at me.

"Do you want to get a drink somewhere?" I asked her.

"Honestly I'd love to but my legs are so sore, I should probably get home and stretch out." She still had the smile on her face, "I didn't want to seem such a wimp in front of Zach. The race this morning really kicked my butt."

I laughed, "You never would have known that. You were so convincing. I can't believe you had any trouble with the run"

"I took two days off after a certain doctor was hit by a car on Saturday."

"Sorry," I grinned as the elevator arrived. We stepped inside.

"It's not that big of a deal. I have until April to get myself ready for the marathon. I'm not looking to win. I just want to have some fun and raise some money."

We arrived on the first floor where I would walk out the hospital and take the commuter rail home and she would go back to her office. I was disappointed that she didn't accept my offer to go for a drink. I was more than interested in Diana. I was about to say good-bye with one last effort to see her again when she surprised me.

"I have a really great bottle of wine and the makings of some great snacks at my apartment if you want to come over," she offered hesitantly

"That sounds great!" I said smiling at her.

"Can you give me about ten minutes to gather my things together in my office?"

"No problem," I said. "I'll hang out over here in the waiting area."

"Ten minutes. Tops," she said hurrying off to the offices within the hospital.

I sat down on one of the couches in the waiting room. I couldn't believe the way things were turning out. Diana had fascinated me since the moment she walked into my examining room in the ER. She was strikingly beautiful in addition to being intelligent. I wanted to know more about her. I wanted to understand her work with the Leukemia and Lymphoma society. I wanted to know who this mystery man was who had the ability to unnerve her so.

Chapter Nine
♥

I walked quickly back to my office. My heart was beating faster than it had when I had run the race this morning. I couldn't believe I had just asked him to come back to my apartment for drinks! What I couldn't believe more was that he had agreed to come. Now what? I thought.

I called Cindy on her cell phone.

"Hey," she answered. "How did the run go this morning?"

"Fine," I answered. "I'm really sore. Those two days of missed training really hurt me more than I thought."

As I talked to her I was throwing some things into my gym bag. I usually walked home in my running shoes from work, but I decided to keep my boots on tonight. I didn't want to make the wrong impression on Steven. I wanted to look my best. It was a vanity that would probably cost me some discomfort tomorrow morning. I lived a short walking distance from the hospital across the Charles River in Cambridge. I wondered if he would rather walk or take the T.

"Listen," I said. "I have to ask you for advice."

"Sure," Cindy answered. "By the way how was dinner with Dr. Ken Doll?"

"Funny you should ask. I just invited him over to my apartment for drinks," I said. Cindy was silent. "Cindy? Cindy?"

"Yeah. It sounded like you said you invited Dr. Ken Doll back to your place for drinks."

"I did. I'm a little worried about it." I confessed.

"Play it smooth and for the love of God, please tell me you have condoms at your apartment just in case."

"Don't get your hopes up in that department, but yes I still have the box you gave me as an apartment-warming present. I just don't want to scare him off."

"Just be yourself. Have a few glasses of wine. Relax and see what happens," Cindy said.

"OK," I answered. I checked my watch. I had about two minutes left. "I better get to the lobby before he changes his mind."

"Good luck," She giggled. "And remember don't do anything I wouldn't do." She was laughing loudly as she hung up.

I grabbed my gym bag, which was abnormally heavy with my sneakers and my laptop inside it, and headed toward the lobby. He was still sitting on the couch he had motioned to when I had walked toward my office. He was reading one of the many copies of *Time* that could be found throughout the lobby. I was nearly standing in front of him before he looked up.

"Are you ready to go?" he asked. I had put my winter coat on and was ready to begin the walk back to my apartment.

"Sure," I said and he stood up next to me. "We have two choices, we can walk there or we can take the T."

"Let's walk," he said, "unless your legs are too sore."

"Not at all. Actually it would be best for me to walk and get the soreness out of my legs."

We walked out the hospital's front door and the security guard called out to me. I waved back. It was just a short walk across the Charles River to Cambridge, and it was a very nice night for November in Boston.

"So," I said, "what did you think of Zachary?"

"He seems to be taking this thing really well."

"He does seem to be taking it well. His parents seem to be doing very well too. I'm more concerned about tomorrow. The first round of chemotherapy can be such a jolt to your system. It is really an eye opener in the cancer process."

"How do you know so much about cancer treatment?" he asked curiously.

"I'm a cancer survivor," I answered proudly. We were actually standing on the bridge over the Charles River. I kept walking but Steven had stopped. I turned to look at him. He was standing there with a shocked look on his face.

"What kind of cancer?" he asked beginning to walk again.

"Hodgkin's Disease," I answered casually. I wanted to be upfront with him from the start. "I was diagnosed when I was thirteen and I've been cancer free ten years this past June."

"That's amazing," he said. "Is that why you do work with the Leukemia and Lymphoma Society?"

I turned to him and smiled, "It's not really common knowledge on the job that I'm a cancer survivor, although I do tell the cancer patients and their families when I meet them."

We were about a block from my apartment at this point. We were walking in silence. I turned to look at him every once in a while. He was looking at me with a mixture of awe and puzzlement. I was happy about that. Sometimes, particularly men, looked at me very differently once they find out I am a cancer survivor

"I have to warn you. My apartment is very small--not anything like that monster new house you have in North Andover," I joked. "I moved in just before you were run down by Mr. Roberts. It's actually temporary. It's a month-to-month rental. I would love to get into a loft a few blocks away, but I have to wait for one to open up. Maybe after Christmas."

We arrived at my apartment. It was the second floor of a three family home. We walked up the stairs to the apartment. There was a living room with a small eat-in-kitchen, a small bathroom, and bedroom. As soon as we walked in, I took his leather coat from him and hung it up in the hall closet. I dropped my bag inside the front door. I walked into the kitchen and grabbed the two bottles of wine that I'd received as a house-warming present. Steven was standing in my living room looking at the pictures on the wall.

"Do you like red or white?" I asked.

"Whatever you want to drink is fine," he answered. "These pictures are great," He said walking over to a black and white photograph of the California coastline.

"That's my brother's photography. He was living in California when he took those," I said.

"He does great work," he said.

I walked back into the kitchen and opened the bottle of red wine. I brought two glasses and the bottle into the living room. I handed Steven a glass and poured a healthy glass for him. I poured myself a glass and put the bottle down on the end table next to the couch, "Please sit down."

He sat down on one end of the couch. I sat on the other side of the couch. I winced as I sat down. My legs were still a little sore. My back and neck were tight as well.

"Still sore?" Steven asked.

I took a sip of my wine and nodded. I rolled my neck from side to side and twisted my back.

"Do you want me to work on your neck?" he offered.

"That's OK. I didn't ask you over to help me with my sore muscles. I'm sure I'll be fine."

"This is when I'm going to insist," Steven said firmly. He got up from the couch and pulled me up with his right hand. He put a throw pillow on the floor and made me sit down on the pillow.

He sat down behind me on the couch, "Do you have a tank top on under your sweater?" he asked.

"Yeah," I answered.

"I don't want to seem forward but, I'll get at your neck and shoulder muscles better without the extra layer of cloth."

"Oh," I said. I thought he was pretty smooth. I took the sweater off. I was sitting between his legs with my wine glass in my hand. He leaned forward and began to massage my neck and shoulders with his right hand. Immediately my muscles began to relax

"How did you end up in Boston?" he asked.

"What version of the story do you want?" I answered, taking a drink of my wine.

"What are my choices?" he asked.

"The long version or the short version," I told him.

"Which one do you want to tell me?" he asked.

"I guess the short version. I moved here after my last boyfriend was transferred with Prudential. We didn't work out, but I grew to love it here so I decided to stay."

"The scotch drinker?" he asked.

I was shocked he had figured that out. "Yep," I winced.

"How long have you been doing work for the Leukemia Society?"

"Since I was in college. I actually have something tomorrow night. I wasn't going to do anything this weekend but one of the girls who is running the marathon with us can't make it to the event tomorrow night. She asked me to fill in."

"What is it?" he asked.

"Don't laugh," I said taking another sip of wine.

"OK, I won't laugh." he promised. He had been steadily working on my neck and shoulders with his right hand. I was thinking about his ability to work out knots in muscles with only one hand. I was so relaxed that I couldn't imagine what he could do with two hands.

"We're going to be guest bartenders at McFadden's."

"Really?" he asked. He stopped massaging my shoulders. I wasn't sure why he had stopped until he had the wine bottle tilted over my glass and was refilling it.

"Thanks," I said. I was beginning to relax.

"Put your head forward," he suggested. I tucked my chin to my chest and he began to work on the muscles in my neck. "Can I take your hair out of the clip?"

I nodded my head and he removed the clip from my hair. My hair was about shoulder length. He began to move his right hand through my hair and massage my scalp.

"Did you lose your hair when you had chemo?" he asked gingerly.

I nodded. I took a sip of wine and explained, "I was thirteen and I thought it was the end of the world. My roommate had lost her hair as well and we bonded over the loss. My hair was actually more of an auburn color before I had cancer. When my hair came back in, it was the bright red it is now. It also began to hold a curl much better."

"So this color is real?" he asked.

I laughed, "Don't you know you never ask if a woman's hair color is real?"

"Sorry. Your hair is the most beautiful color. I know plenty of women who pay very expensive salons to have hair this color and it looks terrible on them. On you, it is stunning. It was one of the first things I noticed about you."

"Really?" I asked turning around to look at him, "What was the second thing you noticed?"

"You play hardball," he said leaning forward. He leaned down and kissed me. It was sweet and short. I could tell he was hesitant. He pulled away from me first and looked into my eyes questioningly. I got up and knelt on the pillow between his legs.

"Do you want to know what I noticed about you first?" I leaned on his legs.

"What?" He asked leaning forward.

"You look like a live Ken Doll, but you don't play by the rules." I said. I had a little buzz from the wine. I leaned forward and kissed him back. Unlike our first kiss, this one had more passion. His lips were soft and he pulled me onto his lap. His left arm, cast and all, was behind my back and his right hand moved up to caress my face. As he moved the hair away from my face, the kiss was quickly becoming very heated. I reached up to put my hand in his hair. He moved his right hand out of my hair down to my left shoulder. His touch was electrifying. I gasped.

He moved his lips across my cheek to my earlobe. He gently pulled it between his teeth and whispered, "Diana." His right hand pushed the thin strap of my tank top off my shoulder as he moved his hand down my arm. I shivered despite the fact that the touch of his hands and his lips were making me really hot.

"Diana," he whispered again in my ear. "Diana, what are we doing?"

"What?" I answered confused. I was sitting across his lap looking into his blue eyes.

"What are we doing?" he asked, his right hand stroking my left arm and shoulder.

"I don't know," I answered. I put my hand up to his forehead and pushed the hair off his forehead as I had that first night. I moved my hand to caress his cheek. I shifted on his lap and he groaned.

"Sorry," I said as I quickly got off his lap. I was standing next to the couch. Steven stood up next to me. With my boots on, my head reached his shoulder. I looked up at him and smiled. I stepped back from the couch but forgot about the pillow on the floor. I tripped and began to stumble. Steven reached out and grabbed me toward him. I came in contact with his chest and put my arms around his waist to avoid falling.

"Thanks," I said looking up at him gratefully. His head immediately came down and kissed me. It was uncontrolled and desperate. His left arm was around my back and his right hand was in my hair holding my head. He kicked at the pillow I had tripped on and began moving walking toward my bedroom. His lips never left mine. I moved with him as he backed me up to the bedroom door.

At the bedroom door, I began to pull his shirt out of his pants and unbutton it. He paused at the door and moved his good arm down my neck cupping my left breast. I pushed him up against the door and began tugging desperately on his shirt. He actually removed his hand from my breast and began to help me with his shirt. Once his shirt was off I couldn't resist touching his bare chest. It was warm, hard, and firm. His arms moved around me and pulled me up against him. I could feel his erection pressing against his jeans and pushing into me. I gasped into his mouth and stepped away from him.

Bare-chested, he leaned against my doorframe watching as I kicked off my boots. I gazed into his eyes as I unbuttoned my jeans and began to pull them down. I stepped out of them and he moved away from the door. As he walked over to me, he kicked off his shoes and unbuttoned his pants. When he reached me, he dropped his pants to the floor. I reached out and touched his bare chest again. With no heels on, his chest was now eye-level. I began to kiss and stroke his chest. He groaned and grabbed my hands. He pulled me toward the bed. He sat down on the bed and pulled me down with him.

I lay back on the bed with my tank top, bra and thong still on. I had pushed off my socks while taking off my boots. Steven sat on the edge of the bed with his boxers on.

He reached down and took off his socks and then turned toward me. "How are your legs?" he asked putting his right hand on my left ankle. "Still sore?"

"A little." I whimpered. He moved his hand up my leg to my calf. He began to knead the sore muscle. I sucked in my breath and I closed my eyes. He shifted and moved his right hand to my right leg. He massaged my right calf. I had my eyes closed and didn't see him move between my legs. His right hand moved up the inside of my left thigh. I jumped and opened my eyes.

"Sorry," I apologized. His right hand continued to caress and knead my thigh. I closed my eyes again. What he was doing felt so good that I couldn't believe it was actually happening.

"Diana," he whispered.

I opened my eyes to find him keeling between my legs, leaning above me. I smiled and reached up to caress his face. I probably should not have had two, or was it three, glasses of wine. He was so beautiful.

"Do you have condoms?" he asked looking into my eyes, his right hand brushing the hair out of my face. He leaned down and kissed me before I could answer. He broke away first.

"Yes," I answered as I reached with my right hand into the nightstand and found the box of condoms Cindy had bought me as a housewarming gift. I sat up and gave him the condom. He sat back on his heels. I looked him in the eyes and pulled off my tank top and bra. I began to push down my thong when he stopped me to take over. I lifted my hips as he slid the silky material off my hips and down my legs.

"Wow!"

"Wow what?" I asked.

"You are definitely more beautiful naked than I thought you would be," he admired.

I laughed. "You thought about what I'd look like naked?"

"Doesn't every man?" He lowered his lips to my navel.

I sucked in my breath. He kissed my stomach and moved lower to my legs. He ran his right hand down my leg and spread my legs further apart. He moved his mouth up my thighs and began to caress me with his fingers. His thumb was rubbing me as his fingers slid in and out of me. I began to breath heavier and my head moved from side to side with the intense pleasure that kept building. Pretty soon I stopped feeling his breath on my inner thigh. Instead his tongue was moving in and out of me. My upper body came off the bed and I reached down into his blond hair. He picked his head up and looked at me.

"Steven," I whispered. He slid up my body to lie on top of me. I pushed his boxers down. In his left hand, immobile from the cast, was the condom. It was then that I realized that he might have some difficulty with the condom. I took it out of his hand and ripped the package open. I reached down between his legs and grasped his penis. He groaned and rested his head on my shoulder. I unrolled the condom on him.

He moved up to lean on his right arm next to my head. He looked down at me and smiled. "Thanks," he said as he kissed me with unbelievable passion. I moved my hands up to cup his face.

He pushed into me and I arched up. "You're welcome," I groaned. I leaned up and kissed the side of his neck. I couldn't think anymore. He was moving slowly with just the right amount of pressure in the right places that I couldn't think. I raised my hips to meet his thrusts. I reached behind him to caress his smooth, muscular back. His lips moved down my neck to my breasts. He bent and took my left nipple in his mouth. I moaned loudly and surprised myself with the sound I made. I had never really been one to make noise during sex but this was different from anything I had ever felt before. He moved from one breast to the other and I was out of control. I remember grasping at his shoulders and back. My fingernails weren't overly long but I thought that I had scratched him. He began to increase his pace and I met him with every push. Suddenly it was upon me. I hadn't ever had an orgasm like it before. My legs began to shake and I arched my back as he sank into to me with the last few thrusts. I screamed and he groaned. He collapsed on top of me.

My breath was coming in short gasps. I realized at that moment that my nails were embedded in his back. His head was lying next to mine. I moved my hands away from his back and he winced.

"I'm so sorry," I said with a blush. "I kind of lost control." He smiled and leaned up to look down at me.

"Not a big deal," he said smoothing my hair away from my face. "I'd much rather have the scratches down my back than this cast on my arm." He lifted his left arm up. "It's rather awkward."

I laughed. "Still. I can't say that I've ever clawed someone before. I feel bad."

"Don't," he smiled again. "Don't all red heads have tempers?"

I laughed again, "I'm usually kind of laid back."

"If you were any more laid back, you would have killed me." He rolled off me and I sucked in my breath.

"Are you OK?" he asked concerned.

"Yeah. Just sore. A little too much exercise in one day," I said. I pulled the sheets up over us.

"Tired?" he asked.

"Yeah. Long day," I answered. "Do you have office hours tomorrow?"

"Yeah, but not until ten. I'm a little useless with this cast." He was lying on his side looking at me. "What about you?"

"I have to be in at nine, but I'll probably get to work between seven and eight to get a run in at the hospital gym," I explained looking up at him.

"Can you wake me up before you go?" he asked. He was stroking my arms.

I was falling asleep. "No problem," I said. My eyes were closing every few minutes. I would open my eyes again to see him watching me. When I would open my eyes, he would smile, lean down and kiss me.

"Sorry," I mumbled, smiling, and closing my eyes. "It's been a really long week."

"It's fine. Go to sleep. There'll be other nights," he said.

"Promise?" I said finally falling drifting off to sleep.

Chapter Ten

☤

"Steven," I heard her whisper. I opened my eyes. She was sitting on the edge of the bed dressed in running clothes.

"I'm going to work. It's seven," she said. "Nice tattoo by the way."

I smiled. I had been sleeping on my stomach and forgot about the anchor tattooed on my left shoulder. "It's from college. It makes my parents crazy." I sat up and rubbed my eyes. "Can you give me five minutes and I'll leave with you?"

"Sure," she said. She walked out into the living room. "Do you want a travel coffee mug?"

"That would be great," I said pulling on my rumpled clothes.

"What do you want in your coffee?" she called from the other room.

"Two sugars and a little milk." I came out into the living room. She had a Notre Dame travel mug waiting for me. She had on black running pants with enough cling in them to remind me of her great legs. She had put her jacket on and had a duffle bag around her back. After handing me the mug she put on a Red Sox Baseball hat.

"Thanks," I said.

"That's my favorite mug. So I'm planning on seeing you again to get it back," she said with a smile.

"Not a problem. What time are you tending bar tonight?" I asked.

"I think we start around nine," she said.

"Sounds like fun," I answered.

"I don't know how to make that many drinks. I'm really hoping people will just order beer," she laughed.

"Thanks for a wonderful evening," I said pulling on my coat. I leaned down to kiss her, but her baseball hat was in the way. I pulled up the brim and gave her a quick kiss. "I'm hoping that's not a sign. I'm a Yankees fan by the way."

"Stranger things have worked out," she laughed.

We left her apartment together and walked across the Charles together quietly. I was drinking my coffee and she had a bottle of water.

"Can you do me a favor?" I asked her.

"Sure," she answered.

"Can you check on Zach today for me and give me a call on my cell?"

"No problem. I was planning to go see him today anyway. I don't think I have your cell phone number."

I reached into my wallet and pulled out my business card. I grabbed a pen and wrote my home and cell phone numbers on the back of it. She took it and slipped it into the pocket of her bag.

"I'll probably call around three," she explained. "Don't expect anything before then."

"Thanks," I said, "for everything. I'll talk to you later." She tilted her hat up. I laughed and leaned down to kiss her quickly. I turned and walked to the T then made my way to the commuter rail line that took me to North Andover.

Around noon, my cell phone rang. I was sitting in my office updating my charts. I assumed it was Diana and didn't look at the caller ID before I answered.

"Hello?" I said.

"Are you still mad about the flowers?" Tommy asked.

I put down my pen and leaned back in my chair and laughed. "It took you long enough to call me back. It seems so long ago."

"Yeah, well I got my ass handed to me by Chelsea," he said.

"Yeah, well I got a broken arm thanks to you," I said.

"Holy shit! Payne didn't tell me he broke your arm! What an asshole!" Tommy was getting upset.

"Payne didn't touch me. What did he tell you?" I said with a frown.

"You knew about the miscarriage. You didn't tell me," he said rather angrily.

"Tommy," I began with a sigh, "I've only known for the last year. It wasn't my secret to tell. To you or to Payne. I was so angry last Saturday that I wanted to put him in his place. I didn't mean to cause problems."

"Actually you didn't cause problems. It helped them a lot. They're OK with it. I'm OK with it. My mom and dad don't know. That's the way Chelsea wants it. She said she'll tell them when the time is right. What happened to your arm?"

"I was hit by a car after I walked out of the Barnes and Noble where I left Payne and Chelsea. I broke my left arm."

"No shit." Tommy said again with a laugh.

"Well I may have the last laugh yet. I met a woman that day," I said smiling at the Notre Dame cup sitting on my desk.

"You got laid," Tommy said still laughing, "That's why you're not mad at me."

He was laughing and I was getting angry. I hung up the phone.

My phone rang immediately. I picked it up and saw Tommy's cell phone on the caller ID. I answered and Tommy was still cackling. I hung up again on him. The phone rang again. I picked it up and answered, "I swear to God Tommy, stop laughing."

"Steven?" Diana asked.

"Sorry," I answered, "my friend Tommy just called and he was laughing at my broken arm."

"Not a big deal. I saw Zach today," she said.

"How's it going?" I asked.

"He's doing really well. I sat with him for a while. He seems really great."

"Good. Maybe I'll stop in to see him tomorrow." I said. "How was your run this morning?"

"Good. I'm not as sore," she said. "Listen I've got to go. I need to work on the memorial service if I'm going to get to McFadden's on time."

"No problem. I'll see you at McFadden's."

"Steven, you don't really have to come. I'd love to see you but it's going to be crazy in there tonight. On top of that they're going to charge a cover at the door. Really Steven….."

"Diana. I want to come. I've been so busy getting everything set up here, I haven't been out all that much in Boston. I'd love to go some place and relax."

"OK," she relented. "Do you know where it is?"

"No. Let me get a pen and you can give me the address." I grabbed my pen. My office phone began ringing. "Go ahead."

"It's one forty-eight State Street. I'll be there between eight and nine. We don't start until nine."

"Listen, I've got to go. I'll see you then and I'll have your Notre Dame cup."

"See you then," she said hanging up. I thought I heard a smile in her voice.

I answered my office phone, "Dr. Edwards."

"OK. I'm sorry," Tommy said. "I didn't mean to laugh that hard."

"Tommy, you're a royal pain in the ass," I said. "I was on my cell phone with Diana and I thought you were a patient."

"Diana," Tommy said. "That's a nice name. Isn't she a Greek goddess of some kind?"

I laughed. "She's a goddess all right."

"She's hot?" he asked. "How old?"

"I'm not sure. Definitely under thirty."

"Aren't you a little old for her?" Tommy said.

"I wasn't too old for your sister." I joked.

He laughed, "So what does she do? Or did you just screw her and not get any details."

"Tommy," I warned. "she works in public relations at MASS General. Its the hospital I was brought to when my arm was broken."

"So that's how it works," Tommy said. "Is she from Boston?"

"No. That's the funny part. She's Canadian." I explained. "She went to Notre Dame and DePaul. Listen buddy. I've got to go. I'll send you an e-mail with details. I'll be home for Christmas. Hopefully without a cast."

I hung up and finished my charts. The afternoon office hours were light. Very few people came in. By five I was happy to leave. One of the nurses commented on my good mood.

"What are you up to Dr. Edwards?" she asked curiously.

"What do you mean?" I asked.

"You're in way too good of a mood for someone who broke their arm a week ago and couldn't go home for Thanksgiving."

"Really? I hadn't realized I was such a grump," I said with a laugh.

"You're not a grump. Just serious," she said. I guessed she had reached a comfort level with me that allowed her to say what she wanted to say.

"Thanks. I'll remember to not be so serious," I laughed again.

I drove back to my house and changed into a pair of jeans and a new shirt. I grabbed my leather jacket and headed to the commuter rail. I had stopped at Dunkin' Donuts and picked up a pound of coffee. I put it in gift bag with Diana's Notre Dame mug. It would take me over an hour to get into the city. I took the train from Andover at seven and then made my way to McFadden's. It was a nice Irish bar. It was about quarter to nine when I arrived. . She had been right about the cover charge. There was a ten-dollar cover charge at the door along with a sign out front that read that half the cover went to the Leukemia and Lymphoma Society.

I walked over to the bar and saw Diana. I couldn't believe what I saw.

There were three young women meeting with the bartender at the end of the long oak bar. They were dressed in identical outfits. They each had on a Team in Training tank top with a short black skirt and black cowboy boots. I couldn't stop staring at her legs. She saw me and smiled. I sat at the end of the bar. The bartender on duty came over. I ordered a Molson. At nine, Diana and the other two girls walked behind the bar. The crowd was growing every minute. She smiled and came over to me. As she approached I saw more completely the outfits they were wearing. The team in training shirts had been pulled into a tight knot at the base of her spine. The tank top neckline had been made lower to reveal quite a bit of her breasts. I was more than surprised. While she had a larger than average chest, she seemed to have more cleavage than I remembered.

"Hey," she said. "Thanks for coming. Do you need a drink?"

"I'm good for now. I brought your mug," I said handing her the gift bag.

"French Vanilla Coffee," she said. "My favorite." As she leaned over to put it on the shelf under the bar, I was treated to a nice view down her shirt. She looked up at me as I was noticing the view.

"I think I'm in trouble tonight," she said tugging at her shirt.

"That's some outfit you have on," I said grinning from ear to ear.

"It was fine until Megan fixed me up." She said tugging at the neckline. "She showed up with padded wonderbras for all of us and a pair of scissors to cut the neckline. I don't think I've ever had this much cleavage."

"You look great," I said. "She did a great job fixing you up. Not that you needed it."

"Thanks," she said. "I've got to get to work."

"No problem. I'll be over here drooling," I said.

She laughed and went to work. The place was filled to capacity. It was mostly young guys at the bar ordering anything and everything they could. Every once in a while Diana would turn my way and smile. I always had a beer in front of me. On more than one occasion the guys bought Diana a shot. Toward the end of the night, I saw her actually throwing the shots over her shoulder. One time she saw me watching and smiled.

At one point, the guy next to me called her over to him, "Hey honey, can I get a bottle of Bud Light and your number?" He shouted at her.

She smiled politely and brought him his Bud Light. She handed it to him and took his money. "What about your phone number?" he asked.

"I'm sorry. I don't give that out," She said smiling at me. I smiled back. I took out my cell phone while looking at her and called her cell. She answered in front of him.

"How's it going?" I asked.

"Pretty well. I'll talk to you later," she said.

I closed my cell phone and smiled at the guy next to me. He walked away rather disgruntled with his Bud Light.

"Thanks," she said. "That's the third time tonight he's asked for my phone number."

"Anytime," I said. "What time do you get done?"

"At twelve," she said.

"Can I walk you home?" I asked.

"No problem," she answered cheerfully going back to work. I was content to sit at the bar and watch her. She flirted with the guys but was never outrageous. Megan, the girl who had "fixed her up", was outrageously catering to all the guys. She was charging extra for the chance to have a body shot. On more than one occasion, she would walk to the side of the bar and offer a body part for a male patron to lick, sprinkle with salt, and then lick again. She then held the lemon in her mouth for them to take. Diana would shake her head and laugh. One of the guys at the bar motioned for her to do the same and she shook her head no and pointed down toward my end of the bar.

She came down to me around eleven, "Do you want something to eat? They're closing the kitchen."

"Will you eat something with me?" I asked.

"If you order some fries I'll come over and steal some," she said. "By the way I've upgraded you to my fiancé. I hope you don't mind. Some of the guys are not leaving me alone. Megan's not helping any by offering body shots."

"You're doing fine," I said. "Order a plate of fries and some chicken wings." I took out a twenty and handed it to her.

Just then Megan came over and introduced herself.

"Hi. You must be Steven," she grinned. She put down two shots in front of us. "Thanks for coming. These are from me and Allison, the other girl."

"Thanks," I said. I was hoping she would walk away so that we could not do the shots. I had way too much beer in me to do shots. She didn't move and we were forced to do the shots. The shot specials that night had been cranberry and vodka as well as Wild Turkey Bourbon. She had been nice to us and given us the cranberry and vodka shots.

Diana grabbed my beer to chase her shot. She made a face. I laughed.

"I hate shots," She said. "I'm way too old for them anyway."

"If you're too old for them, I must be ancient." I cringed. "How old are you anyway?"

"Twenty-five," she said. "My brother Jack had the great joy of calling me on my twenty-fifth birthday to tell me I was closer to thirty than I was to twenty."

I laughed and she walked away to wait on yet another guy. Twenty-five. I figured she was around that, but I was secretly hoping she was a little older than that. I felt like I was robbing the cradle. I had turned thirty last summer and was beginning to feel really old. The crowd at the bar was on the young side. Most of the girls looked older than I'm sure they really were. While I knew they were checking ID at the door, I was sure most of the patrons were hovering around or below the age of twenty-one.

Diana brought my fries and chicken wings over to me. Before she walked away she snatched a chicken wing. I watched her eat it and lick her fingers. That's when I knew I was drunk. I was so completely turned on by her licking her fingers. I ordered a diet Pepsi and prayed I wasn't too completely inebriated. At twelve, the regular bartender got up on the bar and thanked the guest bartenders who waved as they left the bar. Diana came over to me and motioned for me to follow her. The other two girls, Allison and Megan had gone to a back room. She brought me in there.

They had a huge pile of money on a table. Allison and Megan had already started to separate the money into piles.

"Holy crap!" I said. "How much money is there?"

"We're not quite sure. Do you want to help us? We have to be done by close."

"That's less than an hour. Give me a pile," I said. I needed the hour to sober up a little. We separated the money into piles of denominations and then stacks of hundreds. After all was said and done, the girls had raised $1000 in tips and cover charges. Megan had an extra two hundred from her body shot trade.

"Listen," Megan suggested, "I vote Diana takes the money home with her. She lives closest. Steven are you walking her home?"

"I'm going to get us a cab just to be safe," I said. We piled the money in a few take out Styrofoam cases and put them in a plastic bag. It was almost one by the time we had everything all settled. Diana grabbed her gym bag and coat. Her coat was longer than her skirt. She looked down and laughed.

"I look like a prostitute."

"You look fine. I'll go grab a cab." I walked out front to find three cabs waiting. I motioned for her to come outside. We got in the back of the cab.

"Where to?" The cabbie asked.

"100 Cambridge Street in Cambridge." Then she turned to me and smiled, "Thanks for coming tonight. I hope you had a good time."

"I did," I said. "It's been a while since I've been out."

She laughed. "I find that hard to believe. What did my friend Cindy call you? Dr. Ken Doll."

"Who's Cindy?" I said laughing.

She turned red. "She's a friend of mine from when I worked at Special Olympics. She saw you on TV last Saturday and started calling you Dr. Ken Doll."

We arrived at her apartment and I walked in with her after paying the cab driver.

Chapter Eleven

♥

I was a little more than tipsy when we left the bar. I would have been in worse shape had I not started ditching the shots at around ten. Still the shot that Megan had bought me around eleven, along with the beer I had chased it with, were still affecting me. Steven had grabbed us a cab in front of the bar and we were home before I knew it.

I was still embarrassed by revealing the nickname Cindy had given him. She was coming home on Sunday afternoon and I could count on her being on my doorstep demanding details. I definitely had details to tell her. I walked in the door to my apartment with Steven behind me. I couldn't believe I had agreed to wear this crazy outfit to tend bar. The skirt was completely too short and the shirt was completely too low even before Megan took the scissors to it. The cowboy boots were what really put the whole thing over the top.

I took his coat and mine and hung them up in the front closet. I closed the closet door and turned around to look at Steven. He was leaning up against the wall looking at me. I had been refilling his drinks all night long and I was convinced he'd had a little too much to drink as well. I smiled and crooked my finger at him. He pushed away from the wall and came over to me. He put his hands on either side of my head. His cast was resting on my right shoulder.

"Did I tell you how great you looked tonight?" he asked. He was bending down inches from my face.

I shook my head. He took his right index finger and traced the very low neckline of my tank top. I licked my lips and stared into his very blue eyes. He brought his finger up to trace the moisture on my lips. I pulled his finger into my mouth and bit at it. He bent his head and began to kiss me passionately. I reached into his hair and began to suck and bite at his lips. He reached down with his right hand and ran his hand up my left leg. I groaned into his mouth. At the edge of my skirt he pulled it up caressing my leg the whole way. He caressed my bare ass and pulled me into him. I gasped into his mouth and opened my eyes to stare into his.

"Do you know how unbelievable your legs are?" he whispered into my mouth. His forehead was leaning against mine. I shook my head.

He began to move his lips down my neck. He pulled the tank top lower and lower until I heard the rip of the fabric. He was moving his mouth down to my breasts. They were pushed up high in a white satin bra that was about two sizes too small for me.

Surprisingly, he didn't stop at my breasts. He moved lower, to my navel. He licked at it. The Team in Training shirt was bunched around my waist. I shrugged my hands out of the sleeves. My arms were the only things holding it up. It fell to the floor. He began tugging at the short spandex skirt. He pulled the skirt down using both hands. The hard cast was cool against my leg. His right hand caressed my legs all the way down. I was left in my wonderbra, my white lace thong, and my cowboy boots. He moved his hands back up my legs and began pulling down the straps of the T-backed thong. I stepped out of the thong as he spread my legs wider. His lips moved up my inner thighs and my knees began to bend. He began to lick and suck at me the whole time caressing my legs. My hands clutched at his shoulders and head. I couldn't take much more of his tongue inside me.

"Steven," I groaned. Pulling on him. Instead of me pulling him up, I ended up on the hardwood floor of the entranceway. He pulled his head up long enough to smile at me and then moved back up my stomach to my breasts. They were spilling out of the wonderbra and he traced their bulge with his tongue. I began pulling at his pants. He reached into his back pocket with his right hand and pulled out a condom.

I smiled and rolled him onto his back. He was lying on the narrow carpet that lined my hallway. I yanked his pants and boxers down. He had caressed me into a fevered pitch. I tore open the condom and slowly eased it down his penis. He closed his eyes and groaned. I moved up his stomach kissing him. I took each nipple in my mouth and straddled his hips. I eased slowly down on him watching his face the whole time. Each knee was on either side of his hips. He pushed up inside me and I arched my back with the fullness. I leaned over him and began to nip at his lips and lick at him. I moved slowly at first and then more quickly. The straps of the wonderbra were sliding down my arms and my breasts were spilling out more and more with each movement. I was beginning to reach a point of no return. I could feel the spasms beginning. Steven rolled me over onto my back and thrust deeply inside me again and again. We were beyond control, each of us almost at a climax. I pulled my legs up to wrap them around his waist and then realized that I hadn't taken my cowboy boots off. When I pulled my legs up around him, Steven groaned and began to spasm inside me. He kept moving inside me as my hands were pulling at the shirt he was stilling wearing. I began to shake and I let out a scream.

"Wow," he said pushing the hair away from my face, "you still have your boots on."

I blushed, "I forgot I still had them on."

"It's OK," he said, "they definitely made the outfit complete. We could go get in bed any time soon."

I laughed, "I think I have a rug burn on my lower back."

"That makes us even for the large trenches you scratched in my back last night," he said as he moved up off me and stood up. He pulled his pants up and extended his right hand to me to help me up. I grasped his hand and he pulled me up. He held me to him for a moment and he leaned down to kiss me.

I turned to walk down the hallway to my bedroom extremely aware that I was almost completely naked while he was completely clothed. I reached my bedroom and grabbed a nightshirt to put on and finally kicked off my boots. He was standing at my door with his pants zipped but unbuttoned. I had pulled on the silk nightshirt and took off my bra from under the cover of the shirt.

He smiled at me. I was pulling down the sheets and he walked into the bedroom. He came and sat down on the bed. He bent down and took off his shoes and pulled off his pants and shirt. That's when I saw the scratches I had put on his back the night before.

"Oh my God," I said. "I'm so sorry." I was up on my knees and tracing the red lines with my finger.

He turned toward me and lied down in the bed, "It's OK. It's not like its summer and I have to walk onto a beach."

"I'm so embarrassed," I said blushing again. "I don't even want to know the impression I've made on you. This is so out of character for me."

"Which part of this is out of character for you?" he asked.

"I don't fall into bed with guys after knowing them less than a week," I said. "I certainly don't attack them in my front hallway wearing only cowboy boots."

"Just so you know. I'm not exactly acting ordinary," he said. "So maybe my friend Tommy was right. You are definitely a goddess of some kind." He was lying on his right side facing me in the bed.

I laughed, "Diana is the goddess of the hunt or the virgin goddess. I don't think either applies here."

"Can we go on a normal date?" he asked. "Some place I can show you I have self control and that I'm better behaved than an oversexed teenager."

"Sure. I'd like that," I said smiling. "What do you have in mind?"

"Do you want to come up to North Andover and I'll take you out?" He was so hopeful.

"When?"

"Do you have anything planned for tomorrow?" he asked.

"No. I just need to get some work done here first. Final touches on the memorial service," I yawned.

"Is it computer work?" he asked.

"Actually yes along with some phone calls."

"OK. Can I propose a deal?" he asked. I nodded. "Why don't we get up tomorrow and get some breakfast. We can go up to my house. You can do work and I'll do some work too. We'll go out to dinner early and then you can either come home or stay at my house."

"Sounds good. I'll drive us up to your house," I said yawning again. I rolled over and he pulled my back up against his front.

"Whether this normal or not, I want you to know I enjoy spending time with you and I would love to spend more time with you," he whispered in my ear.

"I'm also having a good time, but there's a lot we have to talk about," I said.

"So tomorrow, I promise we can talk," he said.

"Thanks. That would make me feel a lot better about myself," I said.

"Get some sleep," he said kissing my neck. He was stroking my stomach through the nightshirt. I fell asleep in his arms.

Chapter Twelve

♥

It took me a while to fall asleep Friday night. I couldn't believe what was going on in my life. So much of my life had been on autopilot; four years of college, four years of medical school, three years of residency, and then finally my own practice. Here and there, I had relationships. The most serious of them had lasted less than a year and had been with Chelsea Michaels.

Chelsea. It seemed so long ago, but in reality things between us had ended in June when I moved to North Andover, Massachusetts. She had chosen not to move with me to the Boston area. I couldn't blame her. She had an established teaching career and a writing career that was just taking off. She had everything in New York and I was only offering uncertainty in Boston. I tried to convince her to come with me to Boston by asking her to marry me. That had been a disaster. My mother had given me my great-grandmother's engagement ring to give to the "right girl." Chelsea was the "right girl"; she just wasn't the right girl for me. I wanted to make her happy. She was so sad sometimes; so lonely. I was lonely too. That was what brought us together, not love. I realize that now.

What was I doing now? This woman I met by chance was unbelievable. She lived her life with no regrets. It was obvious she had just come out of a relationship with "Scotch Boy." I began stroking the hair at the nape of her neck. She was so full of life and direction. It had been years since I spent this much time with a woman. Even Chelsea and I didn't spend this much time together. I had been to dinner twice with her and went out to a bar with her all in one week. I couldn't remember the last time I had been to a bar like tonight. Now there was the prospect of spending the day with her tomorrow and maybe Sunday too.

I had just turned thirty and it was hard not to think of the future. With Chelsea, asking her to marry me seemed the obvious step to take. I had accomplished everything I had set out to do and now the next step seemed logical. Now I wasn't so sure about my life. I looked down at Diana. I didn't want to get ahead of myself. The one thing I was sure about was that she made me feel good and I'd been laughing more than I had in a long time. I'd been going out more than I had in a long time and I wasn't lonely for the first time in a long time. Even with Chelsea I felt lonely. I resigned myself to have fun and to take it slowly with Diana. I leaned down, kissed her and finally fell asleep.

I woke up to an empty bed. I rolled over to look at her alarm clock. It was after nine in the morning. Propped up on nightstand was a simple note from Diana: "I went for a run around eight. I'll be back by ten."

I rolled over and stretched. I grabbed my pants from beside the bed. I put them on and walked out into the living room. I went to the kitchen and found a bottle of water. I was busy draining the bottle when Diana unlocked her door and came in. She had a bag of groceries with her.

"Morning sunshine," she said.

"How was your run?" I asked.

"Good," she said walking into the small kitchen. "Are you hungry?"

"Starved," I said. "What do you have for breakfast?"

"I picked up a few things," she said. "I wasn't sure what you liked."

"I'll eat almost anything as long as I don't have to make it. I'm not very good at cooking."

"How did you survive college? Medical School?" she said laughing. "How about a cheese omelet with whole wheat toast?"

"That sounds perfect! How far did you run?" I asked.

"Around twelve miles," she said cracking eggs in the bowl and whisking them.

"That's amazing," I commented. "I don't think I could run that long. Around five miles was as far as I could get."

"Do you run?" she asked.

"Not like you," I laughed. "I run on a treadmill at my house in the morning. I started using a rower about a year ago and became addicted to it."

"Is that what the tattoo is all about?" she asked sprinkling cheese on the cooking eggs.

I laughed again, "No. I got that in college after I joined the sailing team at Fordham."

"You sail?" she asked.

"Since I was a boy. My grandfather taught me. By the time I was thirteen I had my own little sailboat. My grandfather passed away about two years ago and left his sailboat to me in his will."

She raised an eyebrow at me, "A sailboat? Where do you keep it? Not in North Andover." She turned back to making toast for our omelets.

"No. It's actually at my grandfather's, well now my parents' house, in Long Island."

"And that's where you're from, Long Island?" she asked.

"No. Actually my parents sold their house in Queens and moved into my grandfather's house in Montauk about two years ago. We used to vacation there every summer. It's kind of weird going out there all the time. I was supposed to go home for Thanksgiving but now I'll go home for Christmas instead."

The omelets were done and we moved to the small table.

"Where did you grow up?" I asked her.

"London," she said taking a bite of her eggs.

"I thought you were Canadian?" I asked confused.

She laughed. "London is a city in Ontario. It's about two hours from Detroit."

I felt pretty stupid. "Sorry. I can honestly say that I know almost nothing about Canada other than Molson beer and that most hockey players come from there."

"We'll have to fix that," she said. She was finished eating her breakfast. "I need a shower. When did you want to head out?"

"Whenever you're ready is fine," I said. I sat down on the couch and turned on the TV. I was flipping around the channels while Diana showered. I was trying to concentrate on the TV and to avoid thinking of her in the shower. She came out of the bathroom in a long white cotton bathrobe with her hair up in a towel.

"What should I wear?" she asked.

I looked up at her and stared at the sight of her in the bathrobe. She was beautiful even in the most ordinary of circumstances. "Casual is fine. Pack something for tomorrow in case you want to stay over."

"OK. A few more minutes and I'll be ready," she said walking into her bedroom.

"It's not a big deal. I'm going to call the restaurant and make reservations. How does seven sound?"

"Fine," she said. She was pulling things out of her closet and putting them on the bed.

I called information and found the number of Orzo a nice Italian restaurant in North Andover that I had gone to with my parents. I made the reservations and sat back again on the couch waiting for Diana. I could hear the blow dryer in her bedroom. When it turned off she came out in jeans and a simple black sweater. I noticed her shoes right away. She was wearing the cowboy boots from last night.

"Nice boots," I said with a smile.

She blushed, "They're actually very comfortable. I'm all set. Here's the problem. My car is at the hospital. I don't have parking here so I leave it at the hospital." Do you mind the walk?

"Not at all. You're the one who ran twelve miles this morning." I said.

"It's actually nice out and I'll enjoy the walk. I'm going to have them put the money from last night in the hospital safe. I don't want to leave it around my apartment." She picked up her duffle bag and I took it from her.

"Let me carry it," I offered.

"I can carry it," she said indignantly.

"Yes, but I'll get all sorts of really bad looks on the street if I'm walking with you while you carry this big bag. Did you bring running stuff with you?"

She blushed, "Yes. I really want to make it through the marathon."

"I'm sure you will." We walked out of her apartment and made our way to the hospital. We were on the bridge over the Charles when I commented about how beautiful the river was in the fall.

"Have you ever been here for the Head of the Charles?" Diana asked.

"No. What is it?"

"It's a gigantic crew regatta in October," she explained. "Teams come from all over the world to compete."

"One of my friends used to row. I'm sure she came for the race in college," I said. I was thinking of Chelsea and how she had rowed in college. She was the one who had introduced me to using a rower.

"It's definitely something to see. Some of the college kids will sit and drink all day watching the races. If the weather is right, it's a great time."

"I'll have to remember that next fall. I spent the last six months setting up everything in my office and then settling into the house. I haven't had a lot of time for anything."

At the hospital, Diana went to security and had them lock up the money from the bar. We walked to her car in the garage. I remembered she drove a Saab. It was a few years old but it was nice. I hadn't remembered her car being a convertible. I climbed in the car and made the obvious comment.

"OK. I have to ask. Why on earth does a Canadian living in Boston have a convertible?"

She laughed, "I've always wanted a convertible and when I finished graduate school two years ago, my dad was getting ready to retire from GM and was able to get a really great deal."

Surprisingly, she remembered how to get to my house from the hospital. We had to stop at the train station to pick up my car. I led her to my house from the train. It was after one when we finally pulled into the driveway.

"Do I get the ten cent tour?" Diana asked.

"Sure," I answered. One thing my mother had insisted I have was a weekly cleaning service. They came every Friday afternoon.

Silently, I thanked my mother because I knew my house would be clean. "I have to warn you that I haven't done as much with my house as I should have."

Chapter Thirteen

I couldn't believe how well maintained his house was. We walked in the front entranceway and he began the full tour of his house. I had only seen his living room and kitchen the first time I was here and that was only for a brief moment.

"This is the living room," he said as we walked into the room to the right off the entranceway. It was a pale sage green with a bay window overlooking the front yard.

"Please tell me you didn't sleep the whole night on that couch last Saturday," I said. While it was large, it didn't look comfortable enough to be slept on for a whole night.

"No," Steven said, "I forgot you came back in that day."

"You were so out of it," I said.

"I woke up at around eleven that night and went up to bed."

We walked into the dining room. There was a small table with a cloth on it with mix and match chairs around it.

"I haven't figured out what I want to put in here yet." Steven said apologetically. "So I bought a spare table and picked up a few odd chairs from a couple of garage sales."

"I like the look of the chairs. If you had the right table it would look great." I said.

He smiled at me and we moved into the kitchen. I remembered it from last weekend. It had dark cherry cabinets with stainless steel appliances. It opened into the family room. The family room had a sectional couch in it with a simple fireplace in the corner. Hanging over the fireplace was a large flat screen plasma television.

"So now you know what I spent all my money on," \Steven joked motioning to the flat screen television.

"A must-have for any man," I laughed. "What about upstairs?"

He led the way to the hallway. I followed him up the stairs to the second floor. The first bedroom was to the right of the stairs. It had a queen size bed, a dresser and a small television.

"This is my guest room," he said. "My mother insisted I have a place for guests to sleep. If you ask me, she did it because she hates staying in hotels."

"I know what you mean. My mom is supposed to come to town in February and I have no idea where she's going to stay."

"In the smallest bedroom I made a home office," he said as we walked to the back bedroom. I was surprised to see a very old desk in the room with books piled all over the floor.

"You need some bookcases," I said.

"Just a few. I haven't gotten that far," he said. "At least I have something in this room." He walked into the third bedroom and opened the door. The third bedroom was vacant.

I laughed out loud. "What do you want to do with it?"

"I don't know," he said.

We walked into the master bedroom and found a beautifully decorated room. He had a king-sized mahogany sleigh bed with a striped blue comforter. The room had been painted a pale shade of blue.

"Wow," I said, "this is beautiful."

"Thanks," he said. "I spent so much time not sleeping during my residency, that I swore I was going to have a great bedroom once I had my own practice."

"Do you really work ungodly hours during residency?" I asked. "I thought television and movies just exaggerated that."

He laughed, "No, it really is terrible. I couldn't wait to be done. When my parents sold their house about two years ago, I refused to get an apartment in New York City. They were too expensive for the complete lack of time I spent there."

"So that's how you survived without knowing how to cook. You lived with your parents."

"Guilty," he shrugged. "I lived at home through college, medical school and then most of my residency."

"Where did you go when your parents sold their house?" I asked.

"I moved in with friends," he said turning away. I felt there was more to the story then he was telling me. He led me into the bathroom. We passed two walk-in closets of the same size.

We walked into the bathroom. His bathroom amazed me. It was the size my bedroom. It had a corner shower and spa tub. There were double sinks.

"OK. This is the size of my bedroom," I said with envy.

"I guess so," he said as he walked out into the master bedroom. "Are you hungry?"

"I could eat a sandwich."

"How's this? I'll order some subs from D'Angelo's and take a shower. You can settle yourself in to do some work while I make myself presentable."

"Sounds good," I said walking down the stairs into the kitchen.

"I have wireless Internet, so you can use your laptop wherever you feel most comfortable." He opened the kitchen cabinet and pulled out the sub menu "What do you want?"

"Turkey with lettuce and tomato," I said.

"No problem," he said picking up the house phone and dialing the sub shop. He ordered my sub and a roast beef sub for himself and then excused himself to take a shower.

The house phone rang about five minutes after he went upstairs. I let it ring and was surprised when an answering machine picked it up.

"Hey Steve. It's Tommy. I was calling to let you know that Chelsea and Payne got engaged this morning. Anyway. Give me a call. I'll see you at Christmas. Good luck with your goddess."

Chelsea. That was the second time I had heard her name. She was engaged. I wasn't as shocked by that as I was by the second part. *"Good luck with your goddess."* Steven had said Tommy called me a goddess. "Your goddess" implied that Steven had laid claim to me.

I took out my laptop and began working on last minute preparations for the memorial service. I had a few phone calls to make to local merchants to confirm orders with them. The florist, the program from the printers, the musicians; everything was set up for the service.

I was catching up on my e-mail when Steven walked into the kitchen. He was dressed in black pants with a cranberry button down shirt. He looked fabulous and smelled amazing. Before I had the chance to tell him about Tommy's message, the doorbell rang and he went to get the door. He came back to the kitchen with the sandwiches in a bag.

"Tommy called while you were in the shower. He left you a message," I informed him.

Steven walked over to the answering machine and pressed play while I started taking the sandwiches out of the bag. While the answering machine was playing, Steven got plates and drinks out for us. At the information that Chelsea was now engaged, he stopped. He put his head down and shook it. He turned to look at me and smiled a forced smile.

"I guess we get to have our first talk," he said to me. He walked over to the kitchen table and sat down.

Chapter Fourteen

Chelsea and Payne were engaged. That's what Tommy had just said. I was upset that she had to hear it, not just the first time when I was in the shower but a second time, when I had pressed play again. I knew she had heard Chelsea's name before and I knew it was time to explain everything to her. I sat down across from her with my plate and my diet Pepsi.

"So I should probably explain everything. Do you remember asking me which version of the story you wanted to hear?"

She nodded.

"Do you want the long version or the short version?" I asked.

"We've got time. Why don't you give me the long version?"

"OK. I met Tommy at Fordham. We had almost nothing in common but hit it off immediately. His younger sister was two years younger and in high school when we started hanging out. Our junior year, she went off to Fairfield University and met a guy named Payne. They dated for two years before he broke things off with her. She had caught him cheating on her after he transferred schools. What no one knew was that Chelsea was six weeks pregnant with Payne's baby. Payne didn't even know. She was so depressed about the situation that she tried to kill herself. She overdosed and miscarried." I stopped to take a drink out of my soda.

"That's what you meant when you said you didn't mean to tell him about the baby," she said.

"When did I say that to you?" I asked frowning.

"You didn't say it to me so much as you said it to Chelsea. You were lying on the couch when I came back into the house to get my keys a week ago. You were really out of it. You called out to her and I walked over to you. You said you were sorry and you hadn't meant to tell him about the baby."

"Is that all?" I asked.

"No. You said you had loved her."

I let out a breath and closed my eyes. "So here goes the rest of the story. Chelsea got herself back together. She finished her degree at Fairfield and found a job teaching while I was at NYU Medical School and then doing my residency at NYU. I saw her every once in a while when I was over at Tommy's house. She was so alone even in a crowded room. I was drawn to her. I saw the same thing in myself. My parents sold their house the same time Chelsea inherited her house from her grandfather. She let me live in her basement the last year and half of my residency. I didn't know about the baby until Chelsea came home about a year ago drunk and distraught. It was October sixteenth, the same day she had lost the baby. I guess she had had a bad day at work coupled with the anniversary of the miscarriage. I was holding her in my arms while she was crying and one thing led to another."

I took another drink from my diet Pepsi, "Once we crossed that line, it was hard to go back. We fell into a routine. Chelsea had been working on a book and finally had it published. I was finishing my residency and had the chance to move up here. I took the chance. She stayed in New York. It really was better that way."

"Did you love her?" She asked quietly.

"Sort of," I admitted. "I loved the idea of having her around. I wasn't as lonely as I had been. She was very understanding of my situation. When I finally bought into the practice, I tried to convince her to move up here. She didn't want to give up her life in New York."

"Was she the friend you were visiting in town when you were hit?" she asked.

I nodded, "I had just come from an awful confrontation with Payne at the Barnes and Noble on Washington Street. Chelsea is Chelsea Michaels the author."

"Wow," she said.

"I'm really very happy for her. She deserves to be happy. He seemed very sincere about caring for her. He swore to me that he was going to marry her.   He said he wanted to marry her because he loved her."

She had been eating her sub the entire time I had been telling her the story.   I watched her for reaction.   She seemed to be all right with what I had told her.

"What about you?" I asked.

"What about me?" she asked back.

"What's the deal with Scotch Boy?" I asked.

"His name's Patrick O'Malley.   He's an executive with Prudential.   We met while I was doing my PR degree at DePaul.   I had just graduated when he was offered a transfer to Boston.   He asked me if I wanted to move with him.   Unlike Chelsea, I agreed and I moved here two years ago," she stopped to take a swig of her diet Pepsi.

"How did that work out?" I asked.

"It was rough.   No one wanted to hire me.   They were afraid of the paperwork that went with my visa.   I went through four jobs before I landed the one at the hospital.   That was about a year ago."

"What about Mr. Scotch?"

"I was hoping we would have a more permanent relationship by now.   What I hadn't realized was that I would get a permanent relationship with him: permanently over.   Beyond having trouble getting a job, I blew my entire savings living in cruddy apartments with terrible roommates. I had promised myself I wouldn't move in with him, but there I was, one year later in Boston with no more money and in need of a place to live. I moved in with him and our relationship spiraled into a steady decline until this past September. I stayed in the house until the beginning of this month when I found the apartment I'm in now."

"Wow. So we're both in the same boat right now," I said.

"Looks like it," she said standing up with her plate in her hand. She walked to the sink and began to wash it.

"Just leave it in the sink," I said. "I'll do it later."

"No I'll do it now. You have a handicap," she said. "How does the water thing work with a cast?"

"I'm telling you now, if my cast is still on at Christmas, I am cutting it off myself," I said.

She laughed, "Doctor's orders?"

"This doctor's orders. You were lucky a week ago. I was about to sign myself out Against Medical Advice when you walked into my exam room."

"You are too funny!" she laughed.

"I'm glad I didn't sign myself out," I said seriously. "I wouldn't have met you."

She blushed.

"I'm sorry. I didn't mean to make you uncomfortable," I continued. The wall clock said almost three. "I've got some reading to do. How much more work do you have to do?"

"Actually, not that much more," she said. "What do you need to read? Charts?"

I smiled proudly, "No actually, I'm teaching a biology class at Merrimack College in the spring."

"Really?" she said surprised. "What made you want to do that?"

"The malpractice insurance," I answered honestly. "The premiums are a killer."

"Sorry I can't help you with the insurance. I'm presently not speaking to my former agent."

I appreciated her sense of humor. "Let me get my textbook from upstairs."

Chapter Fifteen

♥

I waited for Steven come back downstairs with his textbook. He had given me a lot to think about. We had both just gotten out of relationships that maybe we shouldn't have been involved in to begin with. It would be interesting to see how our relationship would progress. I wondered at the idea. Thus far, I was impressed with the way things were headed in our relationship. I was impressed with the attention he had showed me. I wasn't sure, however, if I was impressed because he actually was genuine or because I was so worn down from the lack of attention from Patrick.

We spent the rest of the afternoon working in silence. I was working on e-mails and general things while Steven read the biology text he would be teaching out of in the spring. I was sitting on the couch in the family room while Steven sat in the matching recliner. I hadn't noticed how tired I was and fell asleep with my laptop still on.

I felt a hand push my hair away from my face and heard the whisper, "Diana."

I opened my eyes startled to find Steven leaning over me.

"Sorry. I didn't mean to startle you," he said. "It's almost six. I wasn't sure if you needed time before we headed out to dinner."

I stretched. "Sorry. How long was I asleep?"

"About an hour or so that I noticed."

"Please tell me I wasn't snoring." I cringed at the thought.

"Like a bear," he teased.

I groaned.

"I'm joking," he said smiling.

"How long will it take us to get to the restaurant?" I asked.

"About ten minutes."

"Do I need to change?" I asked. I was still wearing my jeans and black sweater.

"No. That's completely fine," he said. "It's a casual restaurant."

"I'm going to freshen up a little," I said getting up from the couch. I grabbed my makeup bag and headed to the bathroom off the family room.

In the bathroom I checked my appearance. My hair was mussed and my makeup needed to be refreshed. I took my time redoing my makeup and hair. I added a new spray of perfume. When I thought I looked halfway decent, I repacked my makeup bag and moved back into the family room.

Steven had combed his hair and added a sweater for our night out. I couldn't get over how strikingly handsome he was. It was amazing that there weren't women lining up to take him out. We went out to his car. He drove a Volkswagen Jetta. I slid into the front passenger seat. I immediately noticed that his car was stick shift.

"How have you managed to drive with a broken arm?" I asked.

"Very carefully," he explained with a chuckle. "This was why I chose not to go home to my parents' for Thanksgiving. I didn't think I could drive all the way to my parents' house with a cast. I promised them I would be home for Christmas instead."

We were at the restaurant before I knew it. We walked into the restaurant and were immediately seated. Steven ordered a bottle of wine for us and we looked at the appetizer menu.

"Have you been here before?" I asked.

"My parents and I came here Columbus Day Weekend. I order take out from here sometimes and pick it up on the way home from the office."

"Can I suggest something?" I asked.

"Sure," he grinned, "What do you have in mind?"

I laughed at how dirty his question sounded. "My brother Sam is a trained chef. I spent a lot time with him while he was at culinary school. I was kind of a study buddy for him. How about if I teach you how to cook a few simple dishes so that you aren't always ordering take-out?"

"Cooking lessons?"

"If you want," I offered.

"Sure. When do you want to start?"

"Next Saturday?" I proposed.

"Sounds good," he said. "How good do you think I could be by Christmas?"

"You could have probably two or three dishes down by then."

"My mom would die of a heart attack if I cooked dinner for her," he said smiling.

"What do you want to order as an appetizer?" I asked.

"The fried calamari is excellent here," he stated.

"Sounds good to me," I concurred.

The waitress came over and took our order. I ordered veal Milanese and Steven ordered sirloin steak. The wine was excellent and I began to question Steven with my regular first date questions.

"Tell me something about you not that many people know."

"Something not many people know," he repeated thinking.

"It can't be that hard," I said laughing.

"OK. Almost no one knows this. Tommy knows but not that many other people," he stalled. "My mom made me take ballroom dancing lessons in high school."

I don't know if my jaw hit the table, but I was very shocked. I'm sure he could see the surprise on my face. "Wow. Why did she make you do that?"

"My mom's a throwback. She's the consummate doctor's wife. Her father was a doctor. She's gone to Shinnicock Country Club her entire life but is not a member. First she went as a guest of her father and now she attends as my father's guest. She thought the ballroom dancing would come in handy at all the country club events."

"Did it?" I asked. I was a little stunned by some of this information. His parents belonged to a country club. His mother sounded like old money. They lived in Montauk. Most women would have dollar signs in their eyes. I was intimidated by it. My parents were middle class at best. I was wondering how I would fit into his life.

"Not that I noticed. As much as I could dance to the slow songs, there wasn't all that much opportunity to use all the dances I learned."

"I always wanted to learn to ballroom dance," I said, "particularly to salsa or to tango."

"OK. Now may I suggest something? Since you're teaching me to cook, how about some dancing lessons for payment?"

"You've got yourself a deal," I said offering my hand. He shook it. "First lesson next Saturday. We cook dinner and then dance."

"Deal," he agreed.

"How good do you think I could be by New Year's Eve?"

"Depends. If we work at one dance, you should be great," he said confidently. "Why?"

"I'm a bridesmaid in a wedding on New Year's Eve in Chicago." I replied.

"What do you want to learn for the wedding?"

"I guess Salsa. I'm sure I could get them to play something at the wedding," I said.

"Do you get to bring a date?" he asked.

"Yes," I said blushing, "but I was going to just go by myself."

"Will Scotch boy be there?" he asked.

I blushed again. "Actually, I think he is being invited. The bride is a mutual friend."

"Well then I will gladly volunteer to show him what he is missing from his life. The Salsa Queen of Boston." He raised his glass to toast me.

I laughed. We had finished the bottle of wine and were done with our dinners. The waitress came over and Steven paid the bill. I was surprised by the fact that it was almost nine. When I stood up I noticed how much I wine I had consumed. I was a little uncertain on my feet. He picked up our coats at the coat check and we walked out into the fresh air. That helped clear my head a little. We drove back to his house.

When we walked inside, he turned toward me and asked, "Do you want your first dancing lesson?"

"I'm not sure if I'm sober enough."

"Something easy then. A waltz."

"Sure," I conceded. He walked over to the stereo system and picked out a CD. He put it on and came back to take my hand.

"Are you ready?" he asked me. He smiled down and began his instructions.

"So I have a little over a month to get better. What do you think? Do I have a shot?" I asked after we finished.

"I don't know. It may take a lot of work, weekly lessons at the very least."

"When do you want to schedule these lessons?" I asked.

He frowned, "I think you need the intense weekend lessons. Friday night, Saturday and possibly Sundays as well."

"I'm that bad?" I asked.

"No, you're really very good. I'm just shamelessly looking for the opportunity to spend as much time as possible with you." he said his cheeks reddening.

"So I get weekend dance lessons and what do you get?"

"Here's that hardball you play so well," he said smiling down at me. "In exchange for the dance lessons you get to teach me to cook. And I'm warning you, I'm not as talented at cooking as you are at dancing."

"How do you know I'm good at dancing?" I asked.

"You haven't stepped on my feet once, you're following my lead very well, and you have great rhythm."

"Great rhythm? How do you know that?" I asked innocently.

"You move your hips in the most unbelievable way." He said looking down into my eyes.

I met his stare and he bent his head to kiss me. Immediately the kiss was filled with passion. The dance lesson ended as he maneuvered me toward the wall. I began pulling at his belt buckle desperately.

"Oh my God. Diana," he swore as he leaned into me. "I don't know what it is you do to me. I've wanted this all day long." I had his belt buckle undone and had pulled his pants down. He was pulling at my sweater. He pulled it up and over my head. I had a black lace bra on with my jeans. His mouth moved up and down my neck. He pulled my earlobe between his teeth.

"Let's go upstairs," he suggested. He slid off his pants and was standing in his living room in a pair of boxers, his sweater, and shirt. He looked so cute.

"OK," I agreed. I walked past him into the hallway and up the stairs to his bedroom. I walked into his room and stood beside his bed. He walked into his bedroom behind me. He kicked off his shoes and pulled my back up against him. He leaned down and began to kiss my neck. I leaned further back into him. His right hand moved down my arm.

"All day long, I've had to control the urge to make love to you. I swear, you have to be a goddess. You've taken away all my control and turned me into a horny teenager." His left arm was around my waist and his right hand moved to caress my breasts. I arched into his hand and he began to tease my nipple through the lace of my bra. His mouth was at my ear. I unzipped my pants and began pushing my pants and underwear down my hips. He moaned as my hand brushed his leg.

"I need to…" I started to say as his right hand moved from my breast down my stomach toward my pubic hair. "I need to take off my…." His fingers began caressing me. "boots." I finished groaning.

"OK," he said. He moved away as I balanced myself on the edge of his bed and bent over to pull off first one boot and then the next. My pants came off easily and I stood up to find Steven naked behind me.

"Diana," Steven ordered in my ear, "Open your legs for me" His hand was moving down between my legs. His hands slid gently down my stomach and then moved through the pubic hair where he inserted his finger inside me. I fell forward onto the bed with the pleasure the movement of his fingers was giving me. He was standing at the side of his bed with his fingers moving in and out of me; stroking me. I was moaning into the comforter when the pressure of his fingers grew. He fell forward onto me with his hands on either side my face.

That was when I realized it wasn't his fingers moving in and out of me anymore. It was his penis. He was moving slowly withdrawing almost completely and then sinking inside me. He brought his hands to my hips and pulled my hips backward into him. He became more insistent and moved more quickly. He reached down between my legs and caressed me as his speed increased. I was beginning to reach a peak that had me grabbing the comforter and moaning. I felt Steven begin to tense and he pulled out of me. He groaned and orgasmed on my back as he collapsed on top of me.

It was a few minutes before I realized he hadn't worn a condom. Everything had happened so quickly that I didn't think twice about protection. My breathing was beginning to return to normal when Steven rolled to his side and took me with him. He scooted up the bed pulling me with him the whole way.

"Diana," he whispered.

"Hmm," I answered. His right arm was already caressing my bare stomach.

"I didn't quite get a condom on. Is that a problem for you?" he asked shyly near my ear.

I shook my head. "Steven. I need to tell you something." He was caressing my breasts. It was very distracting. "Steven," I groaned.

"Yeah honey?" He was caressing me thoroughly and I couldn't concentrate. I felt my excitement growing again. I was still wearing my bra and he unhooked the back to set my breasts free. He moved his hand down to my vagina. He slid his fingers inside me. "What do you need to tell me?" he asked.

"I can't...." I was breathing fast and he was increasing the speed of his fingers. I moaned shamelessly.

"Tell me," he said rolling me over and looking in my eyes with tenderness. "It's OK."

"I can't have children," I whispered closing my eyes. His hand moved from between my legs to my face and caught the tear that slipped out of the corner of my right eye.

"Look at me," he said, "Diana, open your eyes and look at me."

I opened my eyes.

"Who says you can't have children?"

"The doctors," I explained, "Too many chemicals during a critical time in my development."

"You don't know that for sure," he said with tenderness. "Never say never."

He shifted to lie on top of me. He slowly pushed inside me. I arched up against him, "Do you like that?"

"Yes," I sucked in my breath. I had never had sex without using a condom. It was like nothing I had ever felt before. He withdrew slowly.

"Tell me what you like," he said pushing in slowly. "Do you like it slow?"

I groaned and arched up. His head came down to suck on my nipples. He was sucking so hard on them I thought they would explode. He lifted his head from my breasts and kissed my lips roughly. "Diana."

"Steven," I countered. He was moving faster now and I was arching my hips up at him. He drove in deeper and deeper. I was clutching at him and tightening around him. "Stay inside me. I want to feel you inside me."

He groaned loudly and began to pulse inside me. He shuddered and leaned forward to rest his forehead on mine. He opened his eyes to see me staring into his. He leaned down and kissed me.

"Oh Diana," he said rolling onto his back bringing me with him. He scooted us under the covers and was stroking my back. "They told you the treatment would leave you sterile."

I nodded.

"I'll tell you this. I wouldn't bank on it. You know what doctors do?"

"What?" I asked.

"We *PRACTICE* medicine. It doesn't mean we get it right all the time. It doesn't mean the outcome is what we expect."

"But...."

"Do you keep in touch with any of the other kids that were treated when you were treated?"

"Yes," I said.

"Do any of them have kids?" he asked.

"Yes," I repeated mechanically.

"And you don't think you could have them too?"

I sucked in my breath. I realized it was possible. It was highly unlikely but it was possible. "Steven..."

"Listen to me. There's nothing we can do about it now. Let's wait and see. But maybe we should discuss what we want to do in the future."

I nodded my head.

"Do you have a gynecologist?" he asked. He was stroking my back the whole time.

I nodded my head again.

"I'm sure you've been advised not to go on the pill. They probably talked about the risk of introducing more hormones into your body and the risks for other types of cancer. What about something not involving hormones?"

"Like an IUD?" I asked. I was sure to be as red as my hair. This conversation was entirely too intimate for me.

"Yes. Would you consider seeing your gynecologist to talk about that?" he asked. "Because I will admit that with the amount of times I want to make love to you, condoms are not a really an economically sound investment. I won't lie either. I absolutely love the feel of you without that layer between us."

"I...." I started and buried my head in his shoulder.

He tipped my chin up and looked at me. "Did I embarrass you?"

I nodded my head.

"Sorry. Too many years in the medical profession." He was pushing the hair back from my face. "Do you want to try the IUD?"

I nodded my head. "I'll stop by the clinic on Monday after the memorial service. I'll admit I loved the feel of you inside me. Without a condom. I've never..."

"Never what?" he asked.

"Never had sex without a condom before," I admitted.

"You're a smart woman. I wish I could say the same. But sex with you, I will admit, is the first time I've lost control and forgot to take precaution. In the past, whenever I didn't use a condom it was because I knew she was on the pill. I kind of liked that feeling."

"What feeling?" I asked I was beginning to get tired.

"The feeling of desperate need. The need to be inside you."

Chapter Sixteen

♈

I woke up to find Diana looking down at me.

"Morning," I said to her.

"Good morning," she said.

"What time is it?" I asked.

"A little after eight. What do you want to do today?"

"I don't know. I'd love to make love to you again. Maybe go for a run with you. Have you teach me a really simple dish. Church maybe. Some more dancing." I reached up to pull her down for a kiss. The kiss was quick.

"I can't believe in one breath you said you wanted to make love to me and go to church," she said laughing. "Isn't that a conflict of interest?"

"No. '*Love your neighbor as yourself.*' I think I remember that from school." I said with a wink. I reached up again and pulled her down on top of me. "What do you want to do?"

"I definitely need to get a run in, but I'd love to…" she leaned down to kiss me.

"You'd love to what?" I asked. We were both naked and her body was driving me crazy.

"I'd love to go to church." She said kissing me quickly and then moving to get out of bed.

I grabbed her from behind and pulled her under me. She was giggling. I smiled at her knowingly.

"Hardball again," I said.

"Something's hard," she said pushing her hips up at me.

"And what are we going to do about that?" I asked leaning down to plant a kiss on her neck.

"We could get cooking, and do a little dance and make a little love," she said arching up against me when I pulled her earlobe into my mouth and moved my right hand down to her breast.

"Cute," I said. I moved down her neck from her earlobe and found myself staring at her breasts. I caressed both of them and she arched up into my hands. I bent my head to take her right nipple in my mouth. She sighed contently and I began to suck and lick at her right nipple. I moved to the other nipple treating it the same way while I moved my right hand down caressing her waist. I spread her legs and began caressing her. She gasped and arched again.

"Steven," She whispered with her hands in my hair. She pulled me back up to kiss me. I slid my penis inside her as my tongue slid inside her mouth. She gasped into my mouth and arched up against me. I began moving more quickly as the need to be inside her increased. When her hands moved to my shoulders, I grasped them and pulled them over her head. She was moaning and moving her head from side to side. She was beginning to clench and tighten around me.

"Steven!" She yelled as she began to spasm.

I had my head buried in her neck and groaned as I orgasmed. I heard the yell again, "Steven!" It was more distant than her last yell.

"Steven," she whispered in my ear. "Someone's in your house."

"Steven!" Again the voice called from downstairs, "Are you still in bed?"

I groaned again, "Shit. It's my mom."

"Oh my God," Diana cried trying to wiggle out from under me. I could hear the click of my mother's heels on the hardwood stairs. "She's coming upstairs. Go stall her."

I jumped out of bed and pulled on my boxers. I ran to the bedroom door and arrived as my mom reached the landing at the top of the stairs. "Mom. What a surprise."

My mother was in her early fifties. She was tall, thin and blonde. As always she was impeccably dressed. She had on a black wool skirt with a cream blouse. She came forward to kiss my cheek.

"Your father and I were worried about you. We came up last night and stayed at the Andover Inn. Whose car is in the driveway?" She inquired.

I pulled the door to my bedroom closed. "Mom. I'm not alone." I whispered. I was embarrassed. Diana had already reduced me to being a horny teenager and having my mother show up unannounced at my house to catch me in bed with her proved it. "Can you go downstairs and wait for us?"

She turned on the stairs and laughed. She walked down the stairs laughing the whole time. I went back into my bedroom to find Diana hiding in the bathroom.

"I wasn't sure if she was going to come inside," she said.

"I sent her downstairs," I said. "That's my mom. She thinks she has license to just show up anytime she wants to."

"Steven, my sweater is downstairs in the living room and my overnight bag is in the family room." Diana said. She sounded panicked.

"What happened to the calm cool Diana Goyeau who threatened to sick the reporters on me if I didn't stay for her press conference?" I remarked laughing.

"Steven. It's not the same thing and you know it. I was screwing her son as walked into his house calling his name. I am so embarrassed." She put her head down to avoid my gaze.

I tipped her head up and looked her in the eyes. "Listen. Jump in the shower. I'll get dressed and go downstairs to get your things. Take your time and get dressed. I'll talk to them." I leaned down and kissed her quickly, but reassuringly.

I pulled on a clean pair of boxers, jeans, and a shirt. I grabbed socks and made my way downstairs. My father was in the recliner while my mother was sitting on the couch. My dad had just turned sixty-five and was finally slowing down. He was flipping around the television channels. I grabbed Diana's overnight bag and went back upstairs through the living room. I casually stooped while walking through to grab her sweater and my pants. Diana was in the shower when I walked into the bathroom.

"Damn. I may kill my parents for this stunt. It's going to take all my self-control to go back downstairs."

"Steven. Please. Go downstairs and do damage control," she pleaded with me while I handed her the toiletry bag from her overnight case.

"OK. OK." I walked downstairs and found my mother inspecting my refrigerator.

"Really Steven. You need to go grocery shopping." She scolded as I walked in my kitchen.

"Mom, I'll go this afternoon. What on earth are you and dad doing up here?" I asked. "And why didn't you call?"

"Your mother was convinced that you were moping around and in pain. She wanted to come up earlier in the week but I talked her out of it. I couldn't talk her out of it any longer. Yesterday she insisted to the point I couldn't stand it anymore. We were able to get a room at the Andover Inn for the night and came up last night."

"Listen to me," I warned my mother. "You be good when my friend Diana comes downstairs. She's terribly embarrassed that you showed up here. This is not the way I wanted you to meet her."

"Diana?" she asked. "I don't remember you mentioning her."

"I just met her last week. She works at Mass General."

"Not a nurse I hope," my mother said.

"No mother. She works in public relations."

"Well we were planning to go to brunch at the Andover Inn. Bring her with us," my mother instructed.

"I told you we should have called him and had him drive over." My father was looking at me sympathetically. "Your mother forgets what it was like when we were young."

"Kevin!" she said shocked.

I could hear Diana's shoes on the hardwood of the stairs. "Just be nice to her," I said. "I'd like to keep her around."

Diana walked apprehensively into the kitchen. She looked stunning. She had on black wool pants with an emerald green shirt. It made her skin seem paler and her hair that much redder.

"Hello," She said quietly. I couldn't believe this was the same person who was able to command a press conference.

My father got up from the recliner and came over to her. "Sorry about showing up like this. I'm Kevin Edwards, Steven's father." He shook her hand.

"Nice to meet you, " she introduced herself, "I'm Diana Goyeau."

"I'm Monica Edwards, Steven's mom." My mother said. I could see my mother sizing Diana up. She was taking in everything about her.

"Would you join us for brunch?" my father asked politely.

"Thank you, but I really can't. I have so much more to do for tomorrow's memorial service," she said. I could tell she was nervous. I didn't know what this was all about.

"I thought you had everything set already?' I challenged.

"I need to get back to the office and finalize the details," she answered.

"Can I suggest a compromise?" I said. "Drive me to brunch and then afterward you can leave from there. I'll ride back with my parents."

"I don't know," she hesitated.

"Please?" I begged her. "I'll owe you."

She gave in with a laugh, "Fine."

"Good," my father said. "Let's get going. I'm starved."

I sat in passenger seat of Diana's car. My parents had parked their BMW behind her. She seemed all the more nervous after stepping outside.

"Are you OK?" I asked.

"No," she answered flatly.

"What's wrong?" I asked.

"Let's see. Your parents, who by the way look like they have stepped out of a Ralph Lauren ad, caught me in bed with you. Lord only knows what they think of me right now and I'm about to go to brunch with them."

"Relax. I told them to be nice. My father's really very angry with my mother for this one. I guess she has been nagging him all week to come up to check on me. He finally gave in yesterday. Don't worry about them."

She let out a rush of air, "Am I dressed all right?"

"You look beautiful."

"That's not what I asked. Is this outfit all right?" she asked nervously.

"Diana," I said quiet, "you look fine. What's this all about?"

"I don't know," she answered. "I'm just really nervous.

"Please don't be," I said. "I can handle my parents if they get out of line. I promise."

Chapter Seventeen

♥

I couldn't believe his parents. If Steven was Dr. Ken Doll, his mother was a live Barbie Doll. I had never thought I would see a woman so stunning so late in life. She was tall and slim with blonde hair and Steven's incredible blue eyes. She was so proper. I couldn't believe she had almost walked in on us in bed. If I hadn't heard his mother when I did, she could have walked into the bedroom and found us in bed.

I was very nervous about meeting his parents. They were so wealthy and I wasn't. I was afraid to do something wrong. Steven could tell I was tense about it. He tried to sooth me in the car on the way to brunch.

We arrived at the Andover Inn and went into the dining room. We were seated at a table and immediately ordered drinks. His mother ordered a Mimosa while his father ordered a Bloody Mary. I wanted to have a drink in the worst way. I needed something to relax me but I was afraid to drink in front of them. While we were waiting for our drinks, Steven's mother began the questioning.

"Goyeau," his mother remarked, "that's an unusual last name. Is it French?"

"Yes," I said. "I'm originally from Ontario, Canada."

"Really," she said coldly. I was worried about that *really*. I could see the wheels spinning in her mind.

"Mom, Diana lived just over the border in Canada but went to college in the US."

"Where did you go to school?" she asked.

"I attended Notre Dame for my undergraduate degree and DePaul for my masters."

"How did you end up in Boston?" she pried.

"I had the opportunity to move to Boston two years ago," I said.

"And you're at Massachusetts General now?" she continued.

I nodded as the waitress arrived with our drinks. I hoped that she would start drinking and eating and stop asking me questions. We were given leave to go up to the buffet. When Steven's parents went up to the buffet he held me back. He leaned down next to my ear.

"You're doing fine," he reassured me. "Relax. They'll like you." He kissed my ear quickly.

I smiled tentatively at him and walked up to the buffet. I was very nervous and was worried about eating too much. I was worried about not eating enough. I was worried about eating the wrong things. I was careful about what I selected. I sat down with my plate and waited for round two of the inquisition to begin.

"How did you meet Steven?" his mother asked.

"Diana was the public relations official in charge of my accident." Steven answered for me. "I ran into her at the hospital again on Monday when I was checking on a patient."

"Why was there a public relations person in charge of your accident?" his mother asked.

"The man who hit me with his car was the head of public relations for the hospital. He suffered a massive heart attack and passed away shortly after the accident," Steven explained.

I was happy to have him carry the conversation. I was picking at my food while he was explaining how we met.

"And you had Thanksgiving dinner at the hospital?" his father asked.

"Yes sir," I chimed in, "I was on call all weekend long."

"We had dinner up in Pediatrics with my patient. He was diagnosed with Leukemia on Monday. Diana also does work with the Leukemia and Lymphoma Society."

"Really?" Monica continued her barrage of questions, "What kind of things do you do for them?"

"I do patient relations work as well as fundraising," I explained.

"Diana's running the Boston Marathon to raise money for them," Steven volunteered.

"That's wonderful!" Steven's father exclaimed. "We'll have to make a donation."

"Do you have any events coming up?" his mother clucked.

"I have an art auction in January," I answered nervously.

"That's right up your alley mom," Steven said. He turned toward me to explain his statement, "My mother has an art history degree from Vassar."

"Are you going home to Canada for Christmas?" Steven's father asked.

"No. I'll probably go home at New Year's." I said. "I'm a bridesmaid in a wedding in Chicago. I'm going to try to go home for a day while I'm in Chicago."

"You should come down to Long Island for Christmas," Steven said.

I was surprised by his offer. Apparently so were his parents. His mother almost dropped her glass of champagne.

"I don't know if I'll have the time off," I stammered. "Thank you for offering but I was hoping to spend some time with one of my older brothers. My brother Jack will be in Boston in two weeks."

"Is Jack the chef?" Steven asked.

"No. The hockey player," I said. I had never told him that my brother Jack was a professional hockey player.

"I thought he was a photographer," Steven said puzzled.

"Not by trade. Right now he plays defense for the Montreal Canadiens. He just turned thirty-three and is looking at retiring. He played for San Jose when he took the pictures that you saw in my apartment."

"Are the Bruins playing the Canadiens?" his father interrupted.

"Yes sir, in two weeks during a Saturday afternoon game. I always like those better because I get to go to dinner with him on Friday evening and then go to his game before he leaves town. The night games are more difficult. I don't get to see him except when he plays the game. Usually the team leaves right afterward. He won't be in town again until after the All Star Game."

"That will be nice for you to spend time with him," Steven's mother cooed.

We were finished with brunch and I was feeling very uncomfortable with the whole situation. The quicker I left and got home the better I would feel about the whole thing. I wasn't ready to meet his parents. I wasn't sure I would have ever been ready to meet them. They were from a different world. A world I knew nothing about.

"Thank you so much for inviting me for brunch. It was a pleasure meeting you both. I really should be going. There is still so much more I need to do for the service tomorrow." I stood to get up from the table. I held out my hand to his parents. His father immediately stood and shook my hand. His mother remained seated and shook my hand limply. Steven stood with me.

"I'll walk you to your car," Steven offered.

Steven walked me out to my car. At my car I leaned up against it and turned to Steven. I couldn't figure out what he saw in me. I couldn't figure out how I would fit into his life.

"I'm sorry," Steven apologized. His hand was at my temple pushing back a stray strand of hair.

"What are you sorry about?" I asked holding my breath. Was he sorry he had gotten involved with me?

"I'm sorry my mom is such a bitch," he said.

My mouth dropped open.

"She has this tough layer that she shows to people she doesn't know." He explained. "She's very suspicious of anyone she hasn't known for at least twenty years. I had a great time this weekend. I hope brunch didn't make you rethink our agreement."

"No. Are you coming to the service tomorrow?" I asked.

"If I can get someone to cover my appointments. I'll probably drive in and back. It will save time."

"I probably won't have a chance to spend any time with you."

"I understand," he said leaning forward to kiss me. "Will I see you Friday night?"

"If you still want to," I answered unsure of myself.

"Why wouldn't I?" he asked as he bent down and kissed my lips. It was very chaste at first, but he began to deepen the kiss and lean into me. I couldn't help but respond to him.

"I'll call you this week," he said breaking away from me. "I promise." He trailed his finger over my lips. I turned and slipped into my car. He was standing on the front step of Andover Inn as I drove away.

My phone rang as I left the parking lot. It was Cindy.

"Hey! Where are you?" I asked.

"I'm at your apartment. Where are *you*?" she asked.

"I'm heading onto I93 back into the city." I answered.

"From where?" she asked.

"From Steven's house," I answered.

"Really! Dr. Ken Doll's House." she said shocked. "I'm hanging up and waiting for the story in person. Hurry up and get here!"

I drove to my apartment in Cambridge. I usually don't park my car at my apartment and it took me a good ten minutes to find a spot on the street. I was standing at my front door digging for my keys in my purse when Cindy opened the door.

"Oh my God. What took you so long to get here! I have been waiting in anticipation." Cindy grabbed my overnight bag off my shoulder and pulled me into my apartment.

Cindy was the first friend I made when I moved to Boston. She was originally from outside Hartford, Connecticut. She had gone to Boston College and decided to stay in the area after graduation. She worked for Special Olympics as a social worker. I was impressed by her ability to work with the athletes who were mentally challenged. She was extremely patient and caring. The low pay that came with not-for profit work didn't seem to bother her. She had large amount of money saved up that enabled her to have an apartment in the Arlington area outside Boston. When things between Patrick and I started to unravel, Cindy offered a sympathetic ear, a shoulder to cry on, and then a floor to sleep on. She also helped me find the new apartment.

She sat down on the couch and waited for me to join her. She was blonde and tan with a great sense of humor. She would often have two dates in the same weekend. She was extremely picky about whom she became involved with and most men, she had often mentioned, were not worth her time.

"I'm waiting! Can you hurry up and get your ass in here to give me all the details!" I had stopped in the kitchen to grab two bottles of water.

I sat down on the couch next to her and handed her the water. "So how was your weekend?"

"Great. And yours?" She motioned with her hand for me to hurry up and get going.

"Well. Let's see. I did OK in the road race. I made us over $1000 at McFadden's and had a great brunch at the Andover Inn this morning."

"You are doing this on purpose. I want to know about Dr. Ken Doll and you know that!"

I laughed. "All right! We came back here Thanksgiving night and ended up in bed together. He came to the bar night and walked me home. We ended up having sex in the entranceway. Saturday we went up to his place and we went to dinner and had more sex. This morning his parents surprised him at his house. After almost walking in on us in bed, we went to brunch together where I couldn't quite figure out his mom."

"Holy shit! You whore, you!" she said mocking me. Knowing Cindy and her sense of humor, I knew she didn't mean anything by the comment but I continued to be upset by the situation this morning and paused to look down.

"Di?" she said, "You know I'm kidding, right?"

I wiped at the tears on my face and nodded. "He's really very great. I'm hoping things work out. Dinner was great. He's going to teach me to ballroom dance. He invited me for Christmas dinner and promised to go to Judy's wedding with me."

"So why is it that you are crying?" she asked quietly.

"I don't know. His mother was a total ice queen this morning. She looks like Barbie would look at fifty. I'm worried she has ideas in her head about him and ideas in her head about me."

"How so?"

"Cind. They're ridiculously rich. Steven was on the sailing team at Fordham. He has his own sailboat. They live in Montauk, Long Island. They belong to a country club. It's a little intimidating."

"Who cares how much money they have! Does he make you happy?"

I nodded and smiled, "I had so much fun this weekend."

"Then that's what matters. Listen, I grew up with lots of money, does it matter to me?" she asked.

"No, but this is different. You should have seen her face when he told her I was from Canada and again when he invited me to Montauk for Christmas. What about the fact that my father worked in a car plant? How do you think she's going to react to that?"

"What did he do during brunch?"

"He kept the conversation going. After lunch he apologized for his mother and her bitchiness"

"Then it sounds like you are golden. Did you tell him about Patrick?"

I nodded.

"About the cancer?"

I nodded again.

"About not being able to have kids?"

I started crying again. "He told me I shouldn't count on that. He said," I smiled remembering the words, "doctors *practice* medicine. They don't always get it right."

She looked shocked. "Does he have any brothers?'

"He's an only child." I answered. "The crown prince, so to speak."

"When do I get to meet him?" Cindy asked almost begging.

"How does happy hour on Friday sound?" I answered.

"Excellent. Just one more question before I leave."

"And that is?"

"How is the sex?"

I smiled and took a sip of the water. "Do you want me to rate it?"

"One to ten. One the worst. Ten the best."

I smirked and said coyly, "Fifteen."

Cindy laughed so hard she fell off the couch.

Chapter Eighteen

I turned and returned into the Andover Inn furious with my mother. She had shown Diana her usual aloof attitude when it came to new people in my life. I had seen her do it with Tommy as well as any with any friend that I brought home whose parents were not from "the club". My parents were sitting in the lobby waiting for me when I came inside. After being friends with Tommy for the last twelve years, some of his directness had rubbed off on me. This was one of those times when I was very direct with my parents.

"Can you explain to me why you were so rude to Diana?" I asked.

"Steven really," my mother purred, "lower your voice."

"No. I explained to you that she was very nervous about the situation. Instead of being nice to her, you questioned her like she was an accused criminal." I was angry.

"Steven," my father began, "she's a lovely young woman. If you're still seeing her at Christmas, bring her home with you."

"Fine," I said curtly. I was still very angry but knew that I wasn't going to win this battle with my mother. In fact, the more I argued with her, the more she would be convinced that she was right about Diana. My father was the peacemaker between my mother and me. Throughout my entire life, my mother and I had been at odds particularly over my friends and girlfriends. It was my father that had always been able to bring us back together.

My mother had been born into a prominent family from Long Island. She had led such a privileged life that she was very out of touch with the "common people". She had attended Emma Willard, an exclusive boarding school in upstate New York. She then attended Vassar College and earned an art degree that I have yet to see her use other than to decorate the home she shared with my father and to run charity art auctions. She was a very loving, caring person, but had been raised to be suspicious of anyone who wasn't from her set. I was amazed she had even married my father.

My father was not from her social set, yet she had married him. He had been raised in Bellerose, New York. Bellerose is a small community that straddles the New York City border with Nassau County in Long Island. Most of the residents were middle class and my father's family had been no exception. He had worked his way through college and became an eye doctor. It was while visiting friends in the Hamptons that he met my mother. He had played a round of golf with her father at Shinnicock Golf Club and was later introduced to his only child, my mother. My father fell in love with my mother on sight and convinced her of his bright future and his love for her. He purchased his parents' home in Bellerose. Since his practice was in the city, my mother tolerated the house in Bellerose, but insisted my father join Shinnicock. When she was in a gathering of people she knew, she was comfortable. It was only when she was placed in situations that made her nervous did she revert to the spoiled socialite that she had once been. My father was the one that kept her grounded.

I resigned myself to fight this battle with my mother through my father. He was always able to get her to see things from my point of view. He could put my ideas into my mother's head about Diana. Even though I was thirty, my parents took me grocery shopping before we returned to my house. I was hoping to get a few minutes alone with my father to further explain the situation with Diana but my mother began going through my house making plans for this room and that room.

Finally at around three, they left. I told my father that I would call him this week to talk to him. I settled in to watch the late afternoon football games. At half time I called Tommy on his cell phone.

"Hey!" I greeted him. "What's going on?"

"Did you get my message yesterday?" he asked.

"Yeah. So are you OK with Chelsea marrying him?" I asked.

"Yeah. It's what she wants," he said. "Sorry."

"Don't be. I'm OK with it. Tell her that, would you?" I said.

"No problem. So how is your goddess?" he teased.

"Great," I answered smiling. "She is a goddess. I can't explain it. She makes me laugh. She makes me smile."

"You're fucking kidding me!" Tommy said.

"I invited her down for Christmas," I informed him.

"Are you sure she's ready to meet your mom?" he asked.

"Too late." I answered thinking of this morning's brunch fiasco.

"What do you mean too late?"

"My mother and father showed up at my house this morning around nine and almost walked in on us in bed."

He began laughing.

"Tommy, it's not funny."

"Sure it is. I'm just trying to picture your mother's face. Did she have a heart attack on the spot?"

"Not quite," I said beginning to laugh. "She actually laughed."

"No way. She wasn't the ice queen?"

"No, that came later at brunch."

"Sorry," he said seriously. My mother had been an absolute bitch to Tommy for at least a year. My mother was less than thrilled that my best friend was from a working class family in Astoria. After a year or so, Tommy and his unique charm grew on her. He came out in the summer to the house in Montauk with Julie his girlfriend. After college, Tommy married Julie and I was his best man. Shortly before they were married, Tommy had given up on getting a job in business and had decided to join the fire department. Again my mother was less than thrilled, but instead of being an ice queen to Tommy she treated him as if he were her own son and gave him the earful instead of me for once.

"What did the goddess do?" Tommy asked.

"I could tell it made her nervous. She seemed suddenly very unsure of herself. That was the most bizarre part of the whole weekend. She's in public relations. She's unbelievable at a press conference, yet my mother made her nervous."

"Steve, your mom would make God nervous," Tommy said.

"I'm supposed to go out with her Friday night. She promised to teach me how to cook if I teach her how to dance," I explained.

"If I were you, I'd do something nice for her tomorrow. Your mother may have scared the crap out of her and she may run away."

"It wouldn't be the first time," I said. If my mother didn't like my girlfriend, I could count on the girl breaking up with me within six months. That was how fierce my mother was about my life. "What do you recommend?"

"Hold on. Let me get Julie." Tommy called to his wife. "Julie? What should Steven do for his goddess to convince her to stick around?"

"What happened that she's doubting him?" Julie called back.

"His mother," Tommy answered.

I could actually hear Julie groan. "What does she like to do?"

"Julie wants something to work with. What does she like to do?"

"She's training for the Boston Marathon." I answered.

"Julie. She's a runner."

"Easy," she answered immediately, "a basket of goodies for her like protein bars, foot lotion, muscle relaxing oils and candles. Maybe some bottled water." Julie had recently set up a business where she would put together gifts for people based on what they liked or did for a living.

"Did you get all that?" Tommy asked.

"Yep. Listen I've got to go. I need to get to the mall before it closes to get this together. What are you guys doing for Christmas?"

"We're going to my parents' house in Hicksville."

"Can I convince you to stay overnight there and I'll bring Diana out to meet you the next day?"

"I need to check the firehouse schedule, but I'll figure something out. Good Luck." Tommy said.

"I didn't think I'd need it but now I'll take any luck I can get."

I ran out to the local mall to find most of the things that Julie had recommended. If I had had time, I would have had Julie make up the basket but because I wanted it put together for Monday's memorial service, I had to do it myself. I planned to go to the memorial service and drop off the basket for Diana at the hospital.

Chapter Nineteen

After Cindy left my apartment, I drove myself to the hospital to check on everything for the memorial service and walked home. It was very hard not to be scared about this relationship with Steven. Beyond any problems we experience have as a couple, I felt there would be difficult issues with his parents. When I arrived home I decide to call my brother Jack. He would help me figure out what to do.

"Hey Jack." I said when he answered the phone.

"What's up?" Jack asked.

"I met a guy." I began.

"What's he like?" he asked.

"He's a doctor from New York. He lives north of Boston now. A pediatrician," I said. "I'll bring him to dinner when you're in town."

"Should I get an extra ticket for him for the game?" he offered.

"How many tickets did you get me?" I asked.

"Just two."

"Two is fine," I answered. "Jack, I need some advice."

"Sleep with him Diana," he chided. "You always wait too long to sleep with a guy."

I started laughing. "You're too late. And how very unbrotherly of you. Telling your little sister to have sex with a guy."

"You already slept with him? When did you meet him?" I could hear the shock in his voice.

"A week ago," I said.

"Wow. That's got to be some kind of record for you," Jack noted. "So what do you need advice about?"

"He's really rich and I think his mother hates me."

"You met his parents already? I thought you said he was from New York."

"His parents showed up at his house this morning. Unexpectedly. It was very embarrassing."

He started laughing. "Just be yourself Di. It can't be all that bad. I'll see you in two weeks. I've got to go."

"Bye Jack. Love you."

Monday morning came too soon. I had very little sleep on Sunday night. I was still upset about Steven's parents. I was worried about the service. I arrived early at the hospital to set up all the necessary things. Mrs. Roberts arrived early as well. She was extremely gracious. The service went very well. At one point during the service, I saw Steven. He was dressed in a dark navy suit with a dark navy print tie. He caught my eye and smiled at me. I smiled back. I had been raised to think that all things happen for a reason. Even when I had been diagnosed with cancer, there was a reason for it. I couldn't help but think that Mr. Roberts' death had helped me find Steven. I couldn't help but think that Mr. Roberts was smiling down on us today. After the service was over, Steven came over to me.

"Hi," he said. "You did a great job."

"Thanks," I shrugged. "You made it."

"It seemed only right. I had him to thank for bringing you into my life," he said. "I'm a firm believer of good coming out of bad."

I smiled. He had thought the same thing that I had thought. Great minds think alike.

"What are you doing for lunch?" He asked.

"I was going to order take out and eat in my office."

"Can I persuade you to eat lunch with me?" he asked.

I hesitated.

"Nothing fancy. I don't have a lot of time either. Something nearby." He was trying to convince me. "And I swear no bitchy mothers to grill you *this* time."

I was sold on that last comment, "OK."

We walked to Pizzetta Pizzeria on Cambridge Street and ordered a couple of slices of pizza and sat down.

"Did you get your run in yesterday?" Steven asked.

"Yes," I said, " I drove my car back to work and used the treadmill there."

"When do we start your dance lessons?" he asked.

"Friday night after work I was going to meet friends from the Special Olympics at The Harp by the Garden. Do you want to meet me there and then we'll go dancing from there?"

"Sure. I'll find a place that has Salsa music."

"Sounds good. By the way my brother Jack gave me two tickets for his game next week. Do you want to go with me?"

"I'd love to. I'll warn you that I'm not much of a hockey fan. As a matter of fact, I know very little about it."

"We'll have to change that."

We ate our pizza and then walked back to the hospital where parted ways. Before he would let me go back inside, he pulled me close and whispered in my ear, "I missed you last night. It's amazing how quickly I've became used to sleeping in bed with you." He kissed my ear and promised to call me Thursday.

I walked into the hospital and made my way to my office. In the middle of my desk was a large basket. Attached to the top of the basket was a card. I opened it.

Diana,

Thank you for a wonderful weekend. I'm sorry my parents grilled you yesterday. I'll make it up to you.

Steven.

I began going through the basket. There were a couple of bottles of water, a few power bars, some instant hand warmers, muscle relaxing lotion and candles along with a book of scenic runs in the Boston area.

The phone on my desk rang.

"Diana Goyeau," I answered.

"Diana, its Dr. Cooper. I'm having a meeting at three to discuss the Director of Public Relations position. I'd like you to be there."

"Sure thing." I hung up the phone and was immediately flustered. I wondered what the discussion was about.

I picked up the phone and called Cindy.

"What's up?" Cindy asked.

"Two things. There's a meeting today at three about the PR position."

"Wow. That's huge. Do you think you could get it?"

"I don't know. We'll see what they're going to do. The position was a little vague and out of date. I don't know." I said.

"What was the other thing?"

"I just received a really great basket of goodies from Steven."

"Go Dr. Ken go! What was that all about?"

"Thanking me for a wonderful weekend and apologizing for Mother Barbie."

"Any plans to see him soon?"

"He said he would call Thursday night and then come to happy hour on Friday."

"Impressive," she said.

"He said he missed me last night. The bed was cold and lonely."

"Smooth. I need to meet this guy."

"He's going to Jack's game with me."

At quarter of three, I went to Dr. Cooper's office. I was not surprised to see Terrence and Michelle waiting as well. That was not a good sign. The three of us went into his office and sat down.

"Thank you for coming. As you are aware, we need to revise the public relations position that Mr. Roberts held with us. Within the next week, the position will be restructured and posted. Due to the time of year, the board would like to keep the three of you as acting public relations officers. Since Diana was on call for Thanksgiving, Terrence and Michelle will be on call for Christmas and New Years. We would invite all three of you to apply to the positions that are being created. Please make an effort to devise a schedule that allows for the three of you to be on call from now until New Year's Day. Thank you."

I walked out of the office stunned. I finally had a big break. I was thrilled. I went back to my office and called my parents. My father answered the phone.

"Hi Daddy."

"What's new sweetie?"

"Well. They are restructuring the Director of Public Relations job at the hospital. Basically I can interview and prove myself. Hopefully it will work out and I'll be offered a position."

"That's great! You're due for a break."

"That's not all," I paused, "I met a guy."

"And?" he asked.

"He's a doctor. He's really nice. He's going to Judy's wedding with me."

"By the way. Did you know we've been invited to the wedding?"

"No. She said she wasn't going to do that."

"Well she did and your mom and I decided we're going to go. It will mean a nice vacation for us. Now we can meet your new guy as well."

"Tell mom I said hello. I still have to go for a run today."

"Don't over do it," he warned.

"I won't," I said. They always worried about me. "I love you Daddy."

"Love you too."

I realized I hadn't called Steven to thank him for the basket. I picked up the office phone and called his home phone number. The answering machine picked up.

"Steven. It's Diana. I just wanted to call and thank you for the beautiful basket. Everything in it is so wonderful. It was completely unnecessary. I'll see you Friday at Yhe Harp. Thanks again."

I went for my run at the hospital gym and later walked home with my basket of goodies wondering about my new relationship. It seemed so great right now. I was afraid of what could go wrong.

Chapter Twenty

On Thursday evening, I called Diana at home. It had taken all my willpower not to call her before then. I had received her message about the basket and was thrilled to have had that work out. I had found a dance club in Boston that specialized in Salsa music. Every night I was brushing up on my dancing.

"Hi," I said. "It's Steven."

"How was the rest of your week?"

"Same old stuff," I said.

"How's the arm?"

"Like you said, starting to itch. I have an appointment next Friday at three with an orthopedic at Mass General. Hopefully he'll tell me I can get the cast off before Christmas."

"Did you find a Salsa place for tomorrow night?"

"Yes. Mojitos on Winter Street. They have a group lesson at nine followed by dancing. I thought we could go and take a lesson and then do some dancing. Do you want to come up here Saturday to help me learn my first dish and do some more dancing?"

"Sounds good to me. What do you want to make for your first dish?"

"Something with seafood. That way I can make it Christmas Eve for you and my parents. Are you coming to Long Island for Christmas?"

"I can come if you want me to. If it's OK with your parents. I have off for Christmas Eve, Christmas Day and Boxing Day."

"Of course I want you to come. My parents will be happy to have us. I'll look into the ferry schedule. What's Boxing Day?"

"It's a British holiday that we celebrate in Canada. What ferry? Why do you have to look into the ferry schedule?"

"The fastest way to my parents' house is the New London, Connecticut to Orient Point, New York ferry. Chilly this time of year, but still in service. I think there is a noon ferry that would get us to their house around three. If we had to drive the whole way it would be almost eight hours."

"I'll meet you at The Harp tomorrow at six. It's right across from North Station."

"See you tomorrow."

I called my father after I hung up with Diana.

"What's up Steven?" my father asked.

"I need to talk to you about Diana."

"What's going on?"

"I'm bringing her for Christmas. I really don't want a repeat of brunch. She's a very nice young woman. I need you to talk to mom about this."

"Fine. I'll do it. What can you tell me about her that would make your mother back off?"

"She's a cancer survivor and does all sorts of charity work with the Leukemia and Lymphoma Society. She works hard at her job. She's had a hard time getting a job because she's Canadian and has a visa. She makes me laugh dad."

"If she makes you laugh, that's all that matters. I'll work on your mother."

"Thanks dad." I hung up the phone and looked forward to Friday.

On Friday, everything seemed to take longer than it was supposed to. Finally it was time to go and I left for the train. I arrived around fifteen minutes early at The Harp. I went up to the bar and ordered a beer. I was minding my own business when a very attractive blonde came up next to me.

"Hi," she said eying my up and down.

"Hi." I replied without really looking at her and went back to watching the TV.

"Can I buy you a drink?" she asked, not getting the hint

"No thanks. I'm good." I held up my beer. I tried my best to ignore her but she seemed very interested in me.

"Are you here alone?" she asked.

"No. I'm meeting my girlfriend."

"Oh, sorry. My loss." she said and left me.

Diana walked in at six and immediately came over to me. I bent down to kiss her hello.

"I think friends of mine should be here already." Diana said looking around the bar.

"Who are you looking for?"

"Blonde with hazel eyes." She scanned the bar and saw who she was looking for. "Come on." She said pulling me with her right to the blonde who had hit on me at the bar. I stopped her.

"Diana," I said pulling her back to me, "I met your friend earlier at the bar. She tried to buy me a drink."

Diana laughed and pulled me forward. "Cindy," she called, "did you hit on Steven?"

Cindy burst out laughing and I suddenly felt really stupid. We sat down at the table.

"Sorry," Cindy said to me, "I love doing that to my friends' boyfriends. It helps weed out the creeps."

"Just for the record. I did not tell her to do it. She saw you on TV during the press conference and knew what you looked like," Diana explained.

"I was going to behave myself but you were early and such an easy target. That, and the two beers I already had in me, convinced me I should do it. I'm Cindy by the way," she said holding out her hand to me.

"Steven Edwards," I said shaking her hand.

"So you're the doctor," she teased. "I just wanted to know....."

"Yes?" I said.

"What can I do to mend a broken heart?" Cindy said seriously.

Diana laughed first. I laughed with her.

"Sorry," Cindy said, "I've been waiting all week to use that line."

"Cindy, you work for the Special Olympics?" I asked skeptically.

"Yes sir. I'm a social worker there."

"What made you go into that?" I asked.

"Social Work or the Special Olympics?" she asked back

"Both I guess."

"The money," she said seriously, "I wanted to make boat loads of money."

I was puzzled. Social workers traditionally made very little and non-profit work was very low paying.

"Cindy," Diana began laughing, "He's not used to you and your sarcastic sense of humor."

"My brother is mentally disabled. I've seen some really scary attitudes toward people with mental disabilities."

"Where does your brother live?" I asked.

"With my dad at home in Avon, Connecticut. He's eighteen now and about to graduate from high school." she beamed proudly.

Diana was sitting next to me and updating Cindy on changes at the hospital. I watched her laugh and chat with her friend Cindy. She was so animated and happy. She was wearing a long full black skirt with a turquoise sweater.

"Steven," Cindy called, "do you really know how to ballroom dance?"

"Sure do," I answered. "My mother made me take lessons in high school. I hated her every minute of every lesson but they paid off in the end."

"He's going to teach me how to Salsa," Diana bragged with a smile. "And if he can do that, he is a miracle worker."

"Where are you going to dance tonight?" Cindy asked.

"Mojitos at Downtown Crossing. We have a lesson at nine and then dancing afterward."

"I made sure I wore a skirt and heels so that I could get the feel of dancing with them on," Diana said. "Last time we danced I had on pants and I'll be wearing a big ass bridesmaid dress at the wedding."

I laughed, "I'm sure you'll do fine."

"I need to get something to eat. Do you want anything?" Diana asked me.

"Sure. What do you want?" I asked. "I've never been here so I don't know what to order."

"Why don't we get a platter of munchies to share?" Diana suggested. I nodded in agreement.

"Are you going out to dinner with Jack when he comes to town?" Cindy asked Diana.

"Yes. He has a Saturday afternoon game this time. I think he's meeting me at the hospital Friday afternoon and then we'll go to dinner. The further we are from the Garden when we eat, the less likely someone will recognize him and interrupt dinner," she explained. Diana turned to me and asked. "Your appointment on Friday is at three, right?"

I nodded.

"Do you want to go to dinner with us afterward?" she asked.

"Sure. What time is his game on Saturday?"

"One or two." she said.

"So you get to meet Jack," Cindy said smiling. "Good luck."

"What's that about?" Diana asked. "Jack's not so bad. He's mellowed since he got married last year."

"Let's put some things together. Your brother's wife is in Montreal right?"

"Right," Diana answered.

"And this is a two week road trip?" Cindy continued.

"I guess so."

"And do you have any idea how many penalty minutes your brother has racked-up this road trip?"

"No," she said turning bright red.

"Steven seems a little puzzled. Let me explain. Jack is a defenseman with a tendency to acquire large amounts of time in the penalty box if he hasn't gotten laid in a while. Jack is in the middle of a two-week road trip without his wife and sporting for a fight. If he doesn't get a good fight in this week, he'll be looking for blood from Steven."

"Fair warning," I said. I made a mental note to start following Jack Goyeau's statistics, especially this week.

"Stop scaring him," Diana said. "He's really not all that bad. He just likes a good fight on the ice. He's getting ready to retire soon. In fact, he already likes you."

"How do you know he likes me?" I asked.

She blushed and admitted, "He told me to sleep with you."

I burst out laughing. "Did you tell him you took care of that already?"

"Yes," she said blushing again.

"What did he say about that?" I asked intrigued by a brother that would encourage his younger sister to have sex with a new guy in her life.

"He laughed at me," She said.

It was a little after eight and I motioned for the check. I paid the bill after Diana and Cindy's attempts to stop me. Diana and I got up to leave. Cindy had a date she was meeting at nine so she walked out with us. We grabbed a cab to Mojitos. I leaned over to kiss Diana's neck and whispered in her ear, "I've been waiting all week to dance with you."

"I hope I don't disappoint you," she whispered back.

"I doubt it." I said kissing her.

Chapter Twenty-one

♥

At first I was scared that I had bitten off more than I could chew by trying to learn Salsa in less than a month. We arrived at Mojitos and registered for the dance lesson. It was an hour-long lesson in a large group. It was easy to mess up because almost no one would notice. By the end of the hour, I had some basic steps to the dance down; others I needed to work on. Steven had been very patient during the hour-long lesson. I had stepped on his feet more times than I cared to count. I was very apologetic while he was constantly encouraging me.

After the lesson was over, we went up to bar and ordered drinks. We sat at a table for a few minutes before I asked him his opinion.

"Honestly?" he asked.

"Yes. Please be honest with me. Do you think I can do it?" I asked.

"Honestly. Yes. I think you can do it. You have great rhythm. Are you sure you haven't taken lessons?"

"I took dance lessons until I was diagnosed with cancer." I told him.

"That explains it."

"It was tap and ballet. I was six years old when I started and thirteen when I stopped. That's hardly ballroom Salsa." I said incredulously.

"It's enough. You take instruction very well. Do you want to come back here again next week or do you want to go someplace else?"

"There's someplace else to go?" I asked.

"There's a club in Cambridge that we can try next week. After dinner with your brother?"

"Sounds like a plan. Do you dare try to dance with me on a crowded dance floor?"

"You're too hard on yourself. The problem is not going to be everyone else; it's going to be me being able to control myself. It's a very sensual dance and I've never danced it with someone I was physically attracted to."

I blushed. He pulled me up to dance. True to his word, I didn't think I was doing too badly, but I think it was more that he was an excellent partner. While I could follow his lead easily, he was good at leading. He may have been easy to dance with but he was right about the sensuality of the dance. If I had known how tempting this particular dance was, I would have picked something less arousing. After about an hour of dancing, I couldn't concentrate on the steps any more. I was too busy concentrating on his hands and where they were touching me. At the end of a song, he leaned down and whispered in my ear.

"Can we be done for tonight?"

I nodded not trusting my voice.

"Good. If I don't get you out of here soon, I can't be held responsible for what I might do." He began tugging on my hand. He grabbed our coats from the coat check and we stepped outside.

It had begun to snow while we were in the club so we grabbed a cab for the short ride home to my apartment. I opened the front door and we walked in. Steven immediately pulled me into his arms. He pushed my coat off me and was moving me into the living room. I pulled at his coat until it fell to the floor as well. I reached up under my skirt and pulled off the thick wool tights I had worn with the long black skirt. Steven began removing his shirt and I quickly removed his pants. I gently pushed him back onto the couch and straddled him.

"Diana," he groaned as I eased him inside me, "did you see your doctor?"

"Yes." I gasped next to his lips. I drew his bottom lip between my teeth. He was pulling at my sweater trying to take it off. I broke contact with his mouth long enough to pull the sweater over my head. It was his turn to gasp.

Under my sweater I had worn a black lace bustier. It had been a gag gift from Cindy that I had never worn. I had never had a reason to wear it until now.

"Oh my God. Are you trying to kill me?" he asked, mouth agape. He bent his head and began kissing my neck and pushing the straps down. His lips were at my breasts as I began increasing the speed of my movements.

"Steven," I whispered. He had pulled my left breast free and was pulling on the nipple with his teeth. I couldn't think anymore. He was driving me crazy with his tongue and lips.

He grabbed my hips and rolled me to my back as he lost control. He was moving quickly and I was grabbing at his shoulders. He buried his head in my neck and pulled my ear between his teeth. He groaned in my ear as I screamed. We stayed on the couch for a while; neither of us moving. His lips began kissing my neck and he leaned up to look at me. I had tears rolling down my face.

"Diana," he said quietly, "are you OK?" He was brushing the tears away from my face.

I nodded, again unsure of my voice.

"What's wrong? Did I hurt you?" he asked. His face showed so much concern, I cried harder.

"Tell me what's wrong," he said. He was stroking my face with his hands and gently kissing my tears away.

"It's never been like this," I explained, "Patrick…"

He put his fingers on my lips to stop me from saying any more. "Was a fool," he finished

I shook my head. "He was unfaithful. He said he needed more than I was giving him." I blushed.

"Then he has a serious problem," Steven said. "You have so much passion. I can't believe you wouldn't be enough for anyone."

I smiled weakly.

"Come on," he said getting off the couch and pulling me up with him. "Let's go to bed."

He was completely naked and I was partially clothed. It was a reverse of the last time we were in my apartment. He pulled back the covers and sat on the edge of the bed. He pulled at my skirt and it landed in a pool at my feet. He turned me around again and undid the numerous hook and eye closures of the bustier. The bustier fell to the floor in front of me and Steven traced the lines that ran up my back from the bustier. He turned me around. My hands, previously at my sides, went up to cover my breasts. As intimate as we had been over the last two weeks, there was something about standing naked in front of him that made me nervous. He moved his hands up to take mine away from my breasts.

"Why did you wear that?" he questioned.

I shrugged my shoulders. "I never had a person to wear it for. Cindy gave it to me for my birthday in September."

"I have to tell you that, while you look absolutely breathtaking in it, you don't need to wear that for me. The site of you in anything makes me want you. Hell I can't even look at a pair of cowboy boots the same way again. And right now, I've never seen you look more beautiful."

His hands had been moving up my body as he spoke. I had closed my eyes and felt his lips at my belly. I fell forward onto his shoulder. He pulled me down onto the bed with him and rolled over on top of me. He was leaning over me gently stroking my hair with his right hand. I smiled up at him. He smiled back at me.

"How is it that you haven't found someone to snatch you up?" I asked.

"I don't know," he answered. "Maybe I was waiting for my goddess."

"A goddess. That's a lot to live up to. So when do I get to meet your friend Tommy who called me a goddess?"

"At Christmas," he said and I frowned. "What's wrong?"

"I think your mother hates me," I said as I exhaled.

"My mother hates everyone," he said with a laugh. "Don't take it personally. You should have seen he reception Tommy received the first time she met him. There was more ice in the water than the night the Titanic sank."

"What did she think of Chelsea?" I said. I needed to gauge her attitude toward me by what she had been like toward Chelsea.

He made a face like he was sucking on a lemon and began speaking in a high-pitched voice. "She's a what? A teacher? You know what they say Steven, 'Those who can't do teach.' You can do better than a teacher."

I laughed. "You do an excellent imitation of her."

"Years of practice," he admitted. "Seriously, don't worry about her. I can handle her. I have the heavy gun working on her."

"Who's that?" I asked.

"My dad. He's always able to get to her when I can't," he said with a smile. "Tell me about your brother Jack."

"You'll like him. Don't pay attention to what Cindy said. He was drafted at eighteen to play for San Jose. He's made his rounds in the NHL. He's almost thirty-four and he'll probably retire this season. He and his wife just had a baby boy named John. He's really cute. I'm not sure what Jack will do after he retires. He may finally go to college full time. He's been doing classes every summer. I know he just wants to be in one place. He doesn't really care where."

"And your mom and dad? Tell me about them." He had been playing with my hair while I was talking.

"My dad retired two years ago from the GM plant in Detroit. He loved his job, but they had a buy out and it was too good to pass up. My mom is still working at the local library a few days a week. She loves it and it keeps her sane. My dad likes to tinker with things. You can take the guy out of the factory but you can't take the factory out of the guy."

"And your other brother? The chef. Sam, right?"

"Yes. Good memory. He lives in Las Vegas. He's hoping to open his own restaurant in a few years. He just turned thirty. I was the oops baby. My mom thought she was done having kids when I came along. She always says there's a reason the last is the last one."

"Were you a handful?" he was drawing lines with his fingertips on my arms.

"Most definitely," I said with a laugh. "I was a tomboy with no fear. I was into everything. When you watch your brothers, five and almost ten years older than you, you pick up everything. I played hockey with them. I remember going to all Jack's games.

When I got sick, my parents were crazed. The doctors took them out into the hallway to tell them. My mother fainted. My father cried. They told them I probably wouldn't live to adulthood. Jack did a bone marrow drive in my name. He still does work for kids with cancer. If he's in a town for more than a day, he stops into the local hospital's pediatric ward."

"Do you believe in things happening for a reason?" he asked. "Dare I say, fate?"

"You can't be serious. You're a doctor who believes in fate?"

"I don't know. I just know you and I both ended up in Boston and single. There's just too much that was pure chance." He had moved his hand lower to my stomach. I sucked in my breath and then laughed.

"Ticklish?" he said. "That's something new that I have to store for later."

"Not fair," I said laughing. He was tickling me and I was laughing.

"Do you give up?" he asked pinning me to the bed.

"Yes!" I yelled. "Yes!"

"Yes?" he asked. He stopped tickling me and began caressing me.

"Yes." I moaned.

Chapter Twenty-two

I rolled over at seven the next morning to find Diana staring at me. She had the sheet tucked around her breasts.

"Good morning," she chirped.

"Good morning yourself," I retorted, reaching up to pull her down for a kiss.

She kissed me passionately. "What do you want for breakfast?"

"You," I said.

"That wasn't on the menu," she answered. "I need to get a run in. Do you want to join me?"

"I'd love to but I don't have the clothes or the shoes. Somehow I don't think you would have anything to fit me," I said.

"Why don't you go to store and pick up the ingredients for your first two dishes while I get my run in?" she suggested.

"Did you make a list?"

"I'll do it real quick. Let's get a move on." She was out of bed. I was treated with a great view of her naked body. I lied in bed watching her get dressed. She turned around and chastised me, "Are you getting out of bed?"

"Sure. I was just enjoying the view while I could." I smiled and got out of bed. I dressed quickly. She was at the kitchen table writing a list.

"What am I making?" I asked.

"I have a recipe for tuna filet and one for shrimp."

"Sounds good. How hard are they to make? Remember I'm a cooking virgin," I said with a smile.

"There's no way you're a virgin. Nice try." She laughed. She handed me the shopping list. "I added some things on here for a dessert."

"Yes ma'am," I said taking the list. We left the apartment. She took off on her run and I headed in the direction she had pointed me toward the nearest grocery store.

I wandered around the store filling up a cart with all the things on the list. I added a few things to the cart that weren't on the list. I also added some of my favorite things to eat. Surprisingly I was done shopping and back at her apartment the exact same time she came back from her run. In a way it was embarrassing.

"Wow. I didn't think there was that much on the list," she exclaimed looking at all the bags.

"I added a few things," I confessed. "I'm going to put the perishables in the refrigerator while you shower."

"Good plan. Are we staying here to cook or going to your house?" she asked.

"If you want to dance again tonight, we need to go back up to my house. There's more room there."

Diana quickly showered and dressed. She was wearing another long skirt. This one was emerald green with a white silk blouse. We walked to the hospital to pick up her car. On the drive back I asked about the Public Relations position.

"What did they decide to do about Mr. Roberts' job?"

"They are restructuring it. The main position is Vice President of Public Affairs. Under the Vice President will be Director of Media Relations and Director of Publications. There are also two manager positions. One will manage the Science and Research and the other manages, special projects."

"So what are you going to apply for?" I asked.

"In my dream world, the Vice President position," she said. "In the real world, I would love to have one of the director positions or the manager position."

"I think you should go for the media relations position," I said.

"Why do you think I should do the media relations position?" she asked.

"You forget," I said, "I was at a press conference with you and I saw one you gave on TV. You are great with the media."

"I was thinking of applying for that one or for the Manager of Special Projects," she admitted.

"Manager is beneath you. Who else is applying for the position?" I asked.

"I think Terrence, one of the other people in my position, is applying for the Director of Publications. That's more his field. I don't think he's as comfortable in front of a camera as he should be for the media position."

"Didn't you say there were three of you in the same position?" I asked.

"Yeah. Michelle is the other person. She's *so* much fun to work with," she said rolling her eyes. "Who knows what she's doing. She honestly thinks the top position could be hers."

"Could it?" I asked.

"Not that I can see. She's too self-centered. I don't know what would happen if the two of us went up against each other for the Director of Media Relations."

"You'd get it," I stated confidently.

"How do you know?" She asked.

"I just think you would," I said. "I've seen you in action. I've seen you at the hospital. You know three languages. It doesn't take much thinking to know you're the front-runner. That's what gives you the edge."

We arrived at her apartment and loaded up the car with the groceries and her bag then headed out to my house. It was a quiet ride out to my house. I was lost in my own thoughts most of the drive. I couldn't believe I had only known her two weeks. It seemed to be a lifetime that she had been around. I couldn't imagine not having her around. I loved having her around. She made me smile and laugh, even when she wasn't around.

We arrived at my house and unpacked the groceries. Diana began to see exactly what I had picked up as extras. I had picked up an apple pie and whipped cream for dessert. It was around lunchtime and I immediately picked up the phone to call out for lunch. Diana took the phone from me.

"OK Take Out King, it's time for you to learn to cook," she said.

"Now?" I asked incredulously. "What about dinner?"

"If you do well making the first dish for lunch, I'll take you out for dinner," she promised. "If you don't do well, we can always try again for dinner."

"You are a slave driver," I commented. "Which dish do you want for lunch?"

"How about the tuna recipe?"

"Yes Master. What's first?" I asked. She began lining up the ingredients and pulled out a saucepan. I thought I would watch while she did the work, but I was wrong. She made me do everything. I was mashing garlic and anchovies, adding red wine, and making it boil. I was creaming butter. I was boiling rice. I also made a salad. The one part of this dish that was easy for me was the fact that it involved a grill. I grilled the tuna and before I knew it we were ready to eat. It felt like such an accomplishment. I was beaming at her as we sat down to eat at the dining room table.

I was waiting for her to taste the dish. She sat down and smiled at me. She took a piece of tuna. She ate it and smiled at me again. I smiled back and began eating my lunch.

"You did a great job," she told me. "I think you deserve to go out to dinner. Do you feel comfortable making this or do you want to try something else?"

"I don't know. I could try the shrimp recipe as well. If I know how to make more than one I can offer my parents a choice for Christmas Eve dinner."

"Are we dancing again tonight?" she asked.

"We can dance a little after lunch if you want," I said and she nodded.

"So tell me what I can do to make your parents like me?" she asked.

"I need you to stop worrying about that. I told you the important part," I reassured her smiling. "All that matters is *us*. If I'm happy and you're happy, that's all that matters. I will deal with my parents."

"What should I bring for Christmas?" she asked nervously.

"We'll figure something out," I said getting up from the table. I began bringing dishes into the kitchen. Diana followed me into the kitchen with the remaining dishes. "Do you want to start with a Waltz and then we'll move into some Salsa?"

"Yes sir," she said saluting me.

I walked into the living room and pushed the furniture up against the walls making more room for us to dance. I went to the stereo and put on a Norah Jones CD. We began dancing slowly around the room. It felt natural and right. She was very easily led, but it was more than that. I felt comfortable with her. I couldn't remember ever feeling that way with a woman.

Throughout high school and college, there had been girls that I had dated. They were from the country club for the most part. And for the most part, I couldn't stand them. They were usually more interested in themselves than anything else. They wanted to look good, to feel good, and to be popular. The girls at Fordham were better. There were still the average stuck-up snobs, but there were others that were down to earth. Yet somehow things always fell apart. I know, more often than not, if I liked the girl it was my mother's doing that things fell apart. It wasn't until Chelsea that I wasn't pressured by my mother's interference. Now living in Boston, I had the chance to live my life the way I wanted. Diana was what I wanted.

"Have I told you how wonderful you are?" I whispered in her ear.

She shook her head.

"Well you are wonderful," I said. She looked up at me. I noticed there were tears in her eyes.

"Why does that make you cry?" I asked.

"I don't know," she said. "It makes me happy, but scares me at the same time. I'm afraid it will all fall apart."

"I won't let it," I promised. I was falling in love with her. I knew it but I knew she wouldn't be able to accept that right now. "Do you want to try some more Salsa?"

"Sure," she said. "I think I can waltz. I want to get this dance down. My mom and dad will be so proud."

"Are they coming to the wedding?" I asked as I went over to change the disc.

"They weren't supposed to be coming, but they are. It will save me some time traveling to see them. If they're at the wedding, I won't have to take the extra day to drive out to their house. Instead I'll see them in Chicago."

"I can't wait to meet them." I said. I meant it too. She was so different and I wanted to meet the people that were such a huge part of who she was.

I put on the CD of Salsa music I had picked up earlier in the week. We began to move around the living room. She remembered her steps well and I was again amazed at how well she took direction on the dance floor. Around the second dance I was completely aroused by dancing with her. It was becoming increasingly difficult to concentrate on dancing. My hands were lingering more and more on her. She kept missing her steps. At the end of the song, I gave up trying to ignore her.

I reached down and picked her up against me. She gasped as she felt how aroused I was. I brought my mouth down on her lips. I had my hands on her ass pulling her into me. Her hands were in my hair as she tried to control our passionate kiss. I moved her into the dining room and put her on the edge of the table. I knelt in front of her and moved my hands up her legs. I pulled the tights and underwear down caressing her legs the whole way down. She had her hands in my hair running her fingers through it. I stood up and pulled her into kiss me.

There was so much passion in her kiss I was almost pushed over the edge. I began to fumble with my pants. Finally they fell to the floor and I drove into her. She gasped as I groaned. The table creaked as I leaned into her. She was out of control. Her hips were thrusting up at me. I rolled over and pulled her on top of me. She was straddling me. I thrust up into her as she began to tighten around me. I pulled her down to kiss her as she began to orgasm. As she moaned into my mouth, the table legs gave way under us. She let out a scream of surprise. My ass hit the ground hard as I came inside her.

"Well," I said with a laugh, "can we go table shopping instead of going out to dinner?"

"I can't believe we broke the table," she said laughing.

"That's a first for me," I said pushing the hair away from her face. "I've never broken furniture."

"Don't look at me," she said. "Pretty much everything I've done with you is a first."

"Really?" I said intrigued. I moved and felt the soreness in my lower back. I had absorbed most of the weight when we fell. I winced.

"Are you OK?" she asked.

"A little sore but completely worth it," I said pulling her down for a kiss. "What do you think? Do you want to go table shopping?"

"Sure," she said getting up. She helped me up and I stole another kiss before I swept up my pants and began to pull them on.

"How is it that you completely make me lose control?" I asked of her.

She was smiling at me when I asked. She shrugged her shoulders and gathered up her tights and panties. She sat down on one of the chairs and began pulling on her tights. I stood in front of her and pulled her up again to kiss her. I couldn't seem to keep my hands off her.

"What kind of table do you want?" she asked.

"Something strong," I joked. "You said you knew what would be great with these chairs. What kind of table do you think would work?"

"Something made of old barn wood," she said with a smile. "I think there's an antique place not that far from here."

"What are waiting for? Let's get going," I said eagerly.

We drove to a local antique shop. There we found a beautiful table that was made from an old barn door. Since I couldn't bring it home in the car, I arranged to have it delivered during the week. Then I drove us to a local Chinese place and ordered takeout. We settled in for a quiet evening watching TV together in the family room. We were in bed when I asked her about the statement that had intrigued me all day. *Pretty much everything I've done with you is a first.*

"Diana can I ask you something?" We had just made love and I was leaning over her.

"You just did," she said with a smile. "Do you want to ask me something else?"

"How many men have you slept with?" I asked.

She blushed. "Guess."

"No way. I don't want to put a number on you. If it's too high, I look like an idiot. If it's too low I've insulted you."

"Fine. Five." she squeaked closing her eyes.

"Wow," I said. "I would have guessed you had been to bed with more men than that."

"What makes you say that?" she asked.

"You are *unbelievable* in bed," I said frankly.

"Thank you," she said with tears streaming down her face.

"Why are you crying?" I asked. I hated to see her cry.

"I've never been told that."

"With whom have you been sleeping?" I asked. "You *have* to be joking. I would tell you every time how great you are but I don't want to scare you away."

"You can't scare me away," she promised. "I'm having too much fun."

"Go to sleep before I keep you up all night long having fun and you blame me for missing yet another run."

She closed her eyes and I watched her fall asleep. She was definitely a catch and a keeper. I just needed to keep her around long enough for her to believe me.

Chapter Twenty-three

♥

The weekend with Steven left me believing that what I had found could be for real. Thanksgiving weekend could have been a fluke but there was no way two weekends in a row with him that could be this fantastic. I laughed with him. We made love numerous times. I found myself blushing at the situations I had found myself in and what I had done with him. There was so much sexual attraction between us but it was more than that. I felt at ease with him.

I left Steven at his house on Sunday afternoon. We had gone to Mass at Merrimack College. He was trying to establish himself on the campus for the upcoming spring semester. The table we had found was being delivered on Friday morning. He would come to Boston for his doctor's appointment at three and then go to dinner with my brother Jack and me.

Between Sunday and Friday, I became focused on applying for the newly created position for the Director of Media Relations. I had heard around the hospital that Michelle was applying for the same position. I was at the point with Michelle that I didn't care who actually got the job of Director of Media Relations as long as she didn't get it. I needed to secure something in the hospital in order to keep my visa active. If I didn't secure a position, I would be back at the beginning again, looking for a job that would be willing to take my visa and deal with the accompanying paperwork.

Steven had a busy week getting course work together for the upcoming spring semester. He had called on Wednesday to check in on me. It was a nice feeling to have someone call you for no apparent reason. That's what I loved about this. He was attentive without smothering me. He understood that I needed space to get everything ready for the round of interviews that would follow my application for the new job.

Friday came and I found myself excited to see Steven. I was more excited to see him than my own brother. Jack arrived at the hospital around noon with Sean Walsh, one of the Boston Bruins. I immediately recognized Sean. Several of the Bruins had come to the hospital before and I remembered him from their visits. I took them both upstairs to the pediatric wing. There the kids fell all over them and their celebrity status. I laughed with the kids about the attention they were giving them. To me, Jack was always the older brother who teased me. While Jack and Sean were at the hospital, a TV crew showed up to do a piece on charity work of professional athletes. While I'm sure there would be other people detailed, it was great press for me.

Before I knew it, it was almost four. I took Jack down to my office.

"So when does prince charming arrive?" Jack asked. Jack was built like a typical hockey player. He had broad shoulders and was not too bulky but had enough size to be intimidating. He was sitting in the chair across from my desk with his feet up on the desk.

"Will you stop?" I chastised him. "He should be here soon. We're only going to Harvard Gardens across the street."

He was smiling at me. He had always loved to tease me and this was no different. "His appointment was at three. Barring any problems, that should get him here soon. You'll like him Jack. He's fun. I've had such a great two weeks. He really makes me feel special. He invited me for Christmas at his parents' house and he's going to Judy's wedding on New Year's." I was standing at the door to my office when I saw Steven walking down the hallway.

I smiled. "Here he comes." I couldn't believe how great he looked. He had taken the day off from work and was dressed casually. He had on a pair of jeans with a white dress shirt. Over his arm, he had his leather coat. I couldn't tell if his cast was still on. I would be too early to have it removed, but I knew how much he hated it.

"Hi," I said greeting him.

"Hi yourself." He bent his head to kiss me hello. It was a quick kiss; appropriately chaste in the eyes of the people working with me as well as my brother's watchful eyes.

"This is my brother, Jack," I said motioning to Jack. Jack had taken his feet down off the desk and was moving to stand. Although Steven was over six feet and in very good shape, Jack seemed that much bigger than him. Jack extended his hand.

"It's good to meet you. Now I can put a face to a name." Jack said as he shook hands with Steven.

"What time are our reservations?" Steven asked.

"At four-thirty," I said.

"How far is this place?" Jack asked.

"Right across the street."

We walked out of the hospital to the restaurant. Boston in December can be brutally cold; this day was no exception. Jack and I were used to the cold from the winters by Lake Ontario. Steven, however, was not as prepared for the turn in the Boston weather. We went in and I gave my name to the maitred'. He ushered us to a back corner table that I requested. I always tried to get a table away from the crowd when I went out to dinner with Jack. I did it at Notre Dame, in Chicago, and now in Boston. More than not being disturbed by fans tonight, I wanted Jack and

Steven to have the chance to get to know each other. We sat down and ordered a round of drinks and appetizers. I needed to relax in the worst way.

"So," I said to Steven, "what did Dr. Young say about your cast?"

"I have an appointment Christmas Eve morning to have them cut it off," he announced proudly.

"Isn't that soon?" Jack inquired. "Didn't break your arm at Thanksgiving?"

Steven nodded.

"How long did Sam have his cast on?" Jack asked.

"I don't remember. That was almost twenty years ago," I reminded him. "What made him agree to remove your cast on Christmas Eve?"

"Let's see, I think it was the idea of me taking it off myself if it wasn't removed by then," Steven said with an impish grin.

Jack laughed. "I like you. You've got balls."

Steven laughed at his comment. I couldn't help but laugh as well. "I don't remember you having any fights in the last week. You're in an extraordinarily good mood."

"Next stop after Boston is home." Jack explained. "My wife and I just had our first child in August. It's hard to be away from them for a long time."

"Reason number fifty-six to retire." I said. "Jack's getting ready to retire."

"Retire," Steven repeated shaking his head. "That sounds like fun. I just opened my practice."

"Di says you sail," Jack changed the subject.

"Yes. I can't wait for summer. I'm looking for a place for my boat up here."

"You have your own sailboat?" Jack was astonished.

"Twenty-five feet. It was my grandfather's. When he died two years ago, it became mine," Steven explained. "He taught me to sail when I was thirteen. I've been hooked ever since."

"You should get him to do the Regatta," Jack said to me.

"Regatta?" Steven asked.

"There's a regatta to help raise money for the Leukemia Society," I explained.

"Really? I'll think about it. I had so much fun at the last thing you did," Steven said with a smile.

"What did you do?" Jack asked.

I blushed. "I tended bar with a couple of other girls."

"You tended bar?" Jack asked. "You can't make a drink to save your life."

"She didn't have to make actual drinks. She just had to bend over in front of the customer and he was happy to have any drink she gave him," Steven said with a laugh.

I smacked him. "Not at all fair. You know I had no control over that outfit."

"No control is definitely the way I remember it," Steven said. I kicked him under the table.

Jack burst out laughing. "You *so* need to keep him around. He's a riot! When are you meeting our parents?"

Steven smiled. "New Year's Eve at Judy's wedding."

"By far, you are the best boyfriend that Diana's ever introduced me to."

"Any how many has she introduced you to?" Steven asked.

"Three, including you." He answered seriously.

"So are you first interview or the last interview?"

"I'm the one whose opinion matters the most." Jack said with a smug smile.

"Why's that?" Steven asked. I had been eating my appetizer the whole time enthralled by their banter.

"He's the one who kept me alive," I said. "He was my bone marrow donor."

"Wow. No pressure," Steven responded.

Jack and I laughed. "I can't believe you think I'd really let him hold something like that over my head," I said. "He tries to use it every once in a while."

Steven finally saw the humor in the situation. "You are full of surprises."

We left Harvard Gardens and walked back to the hospital. Jack would have an easier time getting a cab back to his hotel from the hospital in order to be home by the team's imposed curfew. Steven and I could then decide what we were going to do for the night. We arrived at the hospital lobby and walked inside to stay warm. Steven looked like he was freezing.

"You need to toughen up if you're going to make it through the winter," I said. "This is no where near the cold that we have in Canada."

"I can handle the cold outside as long as I have you keeping my warm inside," he said.

Jack laughed heartily. "You really do need to bring him home to meet mom and dad. Dad will love him."

"Have you heard from Sam when he'll be home?" I asked.

"Not sure. Listen I have to get back to the hotel and get a good night's sleep. The tickets will be at the Will Call window under your name," Jack said bending down to kiss my cheek. He turned to Steven. "It was great meeting you. I'm sure I'll see you again. I won't be in town again until after the All Star break. You should come up to Montreal for a long weekend."

Steven shook Jack's hand. "That sounds like a good time. Thanks for the tickets."

Jack jumped in a cab and headed back to his hotel. Steven looked down at me and asked, "What do you want to do for the rest of the night?"

"Didn't you say there was Salsa place in Cambridge?"

"Yes. Do you want to do that?"

"I need the practice. Only two more weeks and I'm on display at the wedding. I just need to grab my bag out of my office." I led him back to my office again. It was almost nine at night and everyone was gone for the day.

I opened the door to my office and walked inside. Surprisingly, Steven walked in behind me and closed the door. He pulled my back into his arms and leaned against the door.

"I've waited all week to touch you and now all evening. I was on my best behavior in front of your brother." He leaned down and began to kiss me. He was wildly pulling me into his arms and then pushing me up against the wall. I responded in kind. He began pulling at my pants. I moved my hands to his pants. I pushed them down while he pushed mine down.

"Steven," I whispered. He picked me up and pressed me up against the wall as he pushed inside of me. He groaned.

"Shh." I warned putting my mouth on top of his.

He continued to push into me. I wrapped my legs around his lower back. He was moving faster and faster. I began to tighten around him. He increased his speed and I was crazed. I began clawing at his shirt, my head tilted back in ecstasy. He pulled my mouth down to his and groaned as he spilled his semen inside me.

"Diana?" Steven whispered against my lips, "Are you OK?"

I nodded my head against his shoulder. He let my legs slide back down to the ground. As they touched the ground, his penis left me and my legs buckled as they had to support me again. I grabbed at his waist. "Sorry." I apologized. I looked up at him.

He smiled at me. "Not a problem." He kissed my lips again. "I still don't understand what it is about you that turns me into an unbelievable wild man. You don't get it do you?"

I shook my head. "Sorry to say I don't. Do you really care?" I asked stooping to pull my panties and pants back on.

"Not really," he said pulling his pants back up. "I missed you this week."

"I missed you too." I said. He was staring intently at me. I wondered what was wrong. "Is there something wrong?"

"No," he said shaking his head, "That's the problem. Nothing's wrong. Everything's right." He pulled me into his arms again and kissed me. "I can't wait until next week."

"Why next week?" I asked breathless from his kiss.

"I can't wait to have this cast off and be able to touch you with both hands," he smirked.

"Are we going to dance?" I asked smiling. "I really need the practice."

"Sure. Let's go to the place in Cambridge. It's right off the Red Line."

"Are you going to be able to control yourself?" I asked.

"In public? I swear." He said raising his hand.

"Scouts honor?" I asked again.

"I wasn't a boy scout," he said. "But, yes, scout's honor. I will control myself while we are out dancing. I can't promise anything else after the dancing"

I held out my hand to shake. He took it and pulled me closer. Instead of shaking my hand, he kissed me passionately.

"Sealed with a kiss," he said with one of his famous smiles. "Are you ready to go?"

"Yes," I said grabbing my workout bag. "Can we stop at my place and drop off my bag?"

"No problem. I actually drove in and have a bag of clothes for tomorrow in my car."

"Leave your car here. Parking stinks at my place. We'll grab your bag out of the car and drop it off on the way."

"You trust me to be alone with you in your apartment?"

"There's not going to be enough time for you to get into trouble."

"That's what you think."

Chapter Twenty-four

Friday night was amazing. Dinner with her brother was fun. He was down to earth and seemed to like me. I was relieved. What I found amazing was that he had met only three of her boyfriends. I imagined it was hard for him to spend time with his family since he traveled so much playing professional hockey. I was going to have to learn more about the game.

Lying in bed with her Friday night, I began to think about things. I could see her drifting off to sleep. She was so passionate and caring. When she led the way into her office, I couldn't stand not touching her any longer. I had never felt that way about a woman before. She was special. She looked up at me as I was stroking her hair. Her eyes were beginning to close. I kissed her lips and pulled her close as I whispered, "Is it bad that I'm falling in love with you?"

"I don't think so," She said yawning. "There are worse things in life than falling in love."

"Like what?" I said pulling her tightly against me and kissing the nape of her neck.

"Cancer," she answered.

"And you've already beaten that," I remarked.

"Hmm." She said. She was finally asleep.

Saturday morning came and she was up early. She kissed me goodbye as she went for her morning run. I went back to sleep and woke up to the sound of the shower. I got out of bed, went into the kitchen, and pulled out a food storage bag to put over my cast. It was coming off in a week and I couldn't wait. I went into the bathroom and pulled back the floral shower curtain to see her rinsing the soap from her hair. She had her eyes closed.

"Morning," she said without opening her eyes. I walked toward her and turned her away from the shower. I ducked my head under the nozzle.

"How was your run?" I asked. She had lathered her bath sponge and began to wash my chest.

"It was good," she said. "Nice baggy. Turn around and I'll scrub your back."

I did as she commanded. "Tell me about the anchor tattoo," she said.

"Junior year on the sailing team I had a bet with another guy. Whoever's lost the race had to get a tattoo. I was so confident that I would win. I had been sailing alone since I was thirteen. With half of a mile left, I slipped and fell overboard. I had managed to grab a line off the boat and was being dragged. The crew had a choice, win or pull me back onboard. They pulled me onboard and I ended up with the anchor tattoo. Rather appropriate, after all."

She laughed. "At least you got to pick your tattoo. My 'tattoo' is the result of radiation treatments."

"Is that what that mark is by your hip?"

She nodded, "Why do your parents hate your tattoo so much?"

"My mother hates it," I clarified.

"Why?" she asked.

"There are a thousand reasons why. There isn't any one reason," I said turning back around.

"Can I ask you a question?" she asked.

"Sure."

She was looking up at me with an intense look on her face, "Are you really falling in love with me?"

"Yes," I said bending to kiss her.

"What's your mother going to say about that?" she asked looking down at her toes

"Who cares?" I said pushing her chin up to look at me.

"I care," she said. "It means a lot to me. I don't want your mother to hate me."

"She won't," I said turning off the water. "Do you trust me?"

"Yes," she said stepping out of the shower. She grabbed a towel and dried off. I stood and watched.

"Trust me about my parents," I said. "I hold all the cards on my mother. You'll never have to worry about her."

"But I do," she said. I walked toward her and pulled her into my arms.

"Do you know what you *should* worry about?"

"What?" she asked, a curious look in her brown eyes.

"You should worry that I won't be able to control myself around your family. It took all I had to control myself last night," I said. I was completely aroused by her. "How much time do we have before the game?"

"Enough," she said as she pulled me out of the bathroom and back into her bedroom.

We fell into bed. I was leaning over her staring into her eyes. She smiled and I leaned down to kiss her. She deepened the kiss immediately. I moved my right hand down her body between her legs. I slid my finger inside her to find her completely aroused. She arched up into me.

"Are you falling in love with me?" I asked.

"No," she answered moving her hands down my shoulders and back. I frowned. "I fell in love with you a long time ago." She arched up her hips and guided me inside her.

I groaned and began moving inside her. I rolled onto my back and she bent over me. She was teasing me by moving slowly while tracing my mouth with her tongue. I grabbed her hips and began pushing up inside her. She leaned back as I drew my legs up to support her back. She began to moan and I rolled her quickly to her back. She was tightening around me. I couldn't wait much longer.

"Tell me," I said into her lips.

"Steven," she groaned.

"Tell me," I demanded pulling completely out of her.

"I love you," she said crying. I sank into her and she screamed. She was crying and I rolled to my back with her lying on top of me. I began to caress her back.

"Shh," I tried to comfort her, "I love you too. Please don't cry." She was crying on my shoulder as I stroked her back.

We lay there for a while. Her tears ended and her body began to shudder. She looked down at me and smiled.

"I'm sorry I cried like that," she said.

"I'm sorry I made you cry. I don't want to make you cry. You make me so happy. I can't stand to see you unhappy."

"Not all tears are tears of sadness," she reminded me. "There are tears of joy too."

"I'll try to remember that," I said. "What time is the game?"

"Twelve." She said. It was ten.

"Do you want to get breakfast first?" I asked.

"I thought you would never ask," she said. "I'm starved."

Diana rolled out of bed and began to get dressed. I lay in her bed watching her get dressed. She pulled on a black thong and matching bra. She took out a pair of jeans from the closet and a simple black v-neck shirt. She turned around and saw me watching her.

"What?" she asked.

"Nothing. I just like watching you get dressed." I said with a smile. "How much are you paying for this apartment?"

"You don't want to know," she said pulling on the jeans.

"Why don't you come live with me?" I asked. She was pulling on the shirt when I asked and I couldn't see her face. When the shirt cleared her head, she was frowning.

"I don't know," she said still frowning.

"What's not to know?" I said getting up out of the bed. She walked into the living room. I pulled out a pair of boxers from my bag. I put them on and pulled out jeans and an undershirt. I followed her into the living room and found her in the bathroom fixing her hair.

"Diana?" I asked. I looked at her refection in the mirror as she was pulling her hair up into a twist and putting it in the clip.

"Can we have this discussion another day?" she asked quietly.

"Fine," I said. "When?"

"After I find out about the job," she suggested.

"How is that process going?" I asked.

"I have an interview next Thursday." She said as she began to do her makeup. She didn't need to wear makeup and on a daily basis I hadn't noticed that she wore much. I only ever noticed some eye makeup and a little lipstick. Still, she was beautiful.

"What comes after the interview?" I asked.

"Christmas," she answered

"You won't hear before Christmas?" I asked.

"No. Between Christmas and New Year's the board will make their decision. The new position begins January 4th."

"Here's the deal. We'll have the 'why don't you move in with me' discussion after January fourth," I said, "when you have the new job."

"You're very sure of me," she said with an embarrassed laugh. She was done with her makeup and hair. I was still standing there in my jeans and undershirt.

"Do we have a deal?" I asked blocking her way out of the bathroom.

"Yes," She said nodding and smiling, "now hurry up and get dressed. I'm hungry and I swore I'd never get involved with a guy who took longer to get ready than me."

I smiled and kissed her quickly. I turned back to her bedroom and grabbed a shirt of my bag. I quickly put it on and pulled on my boots. I was ready to go and we left the apartment. We stopped at a Dunkin' Donuts for breakfast. I had ordered a bacon-egg-and-cheese on a roll while Diana ordered a low-fat bran muffin with margarine. I ordered a coffee and Diana ordered an orange juice. We walked to the T and made our way to the Boston Garden with breakfast in hand She shook her head at me.

"I thought you were a doctor," she chided.

"Only on weekdays," I explained. "I try to eat right Monday through Friday and then splurge only on the weekends."

"Hmm," she said dubiously, "I may need to observe that first hand before I believe it."

"All the more reason to move in with me," I said with a smile. I took a sip of my coffee. We were at Boston Garden and went to the Will Call window. Diana picked up the tickets. As we made our way to our seats, I was impressed with how good they were. We had waiter service at our seats. The game went very well for the Canadiens and not so well for the Bruins.

Between the first and second periods, the waiter arrived with two beers for us. We hadn't ordered them and were puzzled by their arrival. "They're from the gentleman in section eleven."

We turned to look at the section and Diana went pale. It was Scotch boy. He raised his glass to us again.

"Do you want me to go talk to him?" I asked. I didn't like to see her so upset.

"No," she said, "I'm going to take care of this once and for all." She got up to walk back to him. I started to follow her and she stopped me. "Don't. I need to handle this."

I watched as she walked up the steps to his level. He began to get up and she pushed him back down into his seat. Her face became red as she was firmly explaining something to him. He nodded and she turned to return down the steps to me. She was smiling.

"All taken care of," she said sitting back down again. She picked up the beer and began to drink it. "No sense in wasting good beer."

I took a sip of the beer and returned my attention to the game. I glanced over my shoulder at one point and saw Scotch boy get up out of his seat.

"I'm going up to the restroom." I said.

She nodded engrossed in the game.

I followed Scotch Boy into the bathroom. I waited for him by the sinks.

"Patrick, right?" I asked him.

"Yeah," he grunted.

"Thanks for the beer but I think it would be best if you just left Diana alone." I said.

"I've had this discussion with her already," he said turning away from me.

"And now you've had it with me," I said stepping in front of him. "Leave her alone."

"Fine," he said walking around me.

I left the men's room and returned to my seat. Diana was still engrossed in the game. After the second intermission, the Bruins were losing four to one and most of the crowd had left, including Scotch boy. With two minutes left to play, an usher met us at our seats. He escorted us to ice level and we waited for Jack to come off the ice. A couple of the guys greeted and nodded to Diana as they passed by.

Jack stopped to speak to us briefly. He went into the locker room and we waited outside for him to be finished with the team. I took the time to ask her about Patrick.

"What did you say to Patrick?" I asked.

She smiled a devilish grin that I had yet to see, "I told him if he didn't stop bothering me I'd have to start telling people all the sordid little details about him that he didn't think I knew."

"You played hardball with him?"

"The hardest!" she said laughing.

"Now you have me intrigued," I said almost pleading with her to continue.

"Let's put it this way. When Patrick and I broke up in September, I knew he had been unfaithful. It wasn't until the end of October that I found out some details. I came across some pictures and an e-mail he had printed and left out. It was almost as if he had wanted me to know."

"What were the pictures of?" I asked.

"They were rather dirty pictures with a rather descriptive e-mail," she said. "Apparently he met up with a dominatrix sometime last summer and had a few sessions with her."

I was shocked. Apparently my faced showed it. She began to laugh.

"Exactly how I reacted. Then I was angry with him. I stashed one of the pictures and photocopied the e-mail. I began looking for an apartment immediately. I slept on Cindy's floor a few nights."

"Is that why you don't want to move in with me?" I asked.

"Steven," she frowned, "please don't push me. I need time. I just came out of a really bad situation."

"I'm not pushing Diana," I said with a sigh. "I'm just trying to figure things out." I pulled her into my arms and caressed her back. I began to sway with her as if we were dancing.

"Do you want to go dancing?" she asked.

"I love to dance with you," I said. "Do you want to go?"

"For a little while maybe. I'm tired tonight," she said.

Jack came out of the locker room and we walked with him to the team bus. At the bus, he signed a few autographs. When he was done, he stooped and hugged Diana. He picked her up and kissed her like a little girl.

"Take care of yourself," he advised. "Don't run too hard. I'll call you soon."

Jack turned to me and shook my hand. "Make sure she doesn't do anything crazy. You need to come to Canada for a weekend."

"I'd love to," I said.

Jack got on the bus and Diana, eyes gleaming with tears, smiled at me after she wiped away the tears. I pulled her to me and kissed her forehead. Jack waved at us again as he settled into his seat.

"Let's go get some dancing in," I said smiling at her.

Chapter Twenty-Five

♥

Thursday morning I was so nervous I woke up and immediately began vomiting. I wanted this job so badly. I wanted the stability that came with the position. I wanted the increased salary. I wanted it because I had earned it.

I reported to work as usual. I had chosen to skip my run that morning. If the interview went well I would go for a run later when my stomach had settled. My parents had called the night before. Cindy had called as well. Steven went one step farther. He sent me flowers at work. It was a bouquet of purple flowers. I don't know how he had figured out my favorite color.

The card had read: *Good Luck! I love you, Steven.*

I arrived at work on Thursday and smiled at the flowers that greeted me on my desk. The interview was at ten. The phone rang. I saw from the caller ID that it was Steven.

"Hi," I said answering my phone informally.

"I was just calling to wish you luck again. Although I know you don't need it," he said. "What do you want to bet that you get the job?"

"I don't know," I said. "There isn't anything I really want."

"I'll think of something for you," he said. "I want a weekend in Vegas."

"Why Vegas?" I asked.

"I want to meet Sam," he explained.

I smiled. "I know what I want. I want a sunset sail."

"You don't have to bet me for that. Are you nervous?"

"Yeah. I puked this morning I was so nervous. I skipped my run." I said.

"Are you OK?" he asked.

"I'm fine." I said. I looked at the clock. It was nine thirty. "Listen I had better get going. Thanks for calling."

"I love you," he said.

"I love you too," I said. It had taken me most of the week to get used to saying it to him.

The interview went well. I left confident that I had left a positive and lasting impression. Michelle was the next candidate to be interviewed. She was waiting as I came out of the boardroom. She smirked at me. She was so confident that she would get the position. I smiled back and went back to my office. The phone rang at noon. It was Steven.

"How did it go?"

"I think it went pretty well. Michelle was waiting for her interview when I came out. As I predicted, she was rather confident that she was going to end up with the job."

"Listen, I have that appointment at the hospital tomorrow morning. Can I drive to the hospital tonight and we'll leave for my parents' after I get my cast off."

"I still need to get something for your parents for Christmas. Can you suggest something?" I asked.

"How about this?" he suggested. "I'll meet you at the hospital tonight and we'll go out shopping for something."

"OK," I said. "I'd better get some work done if you're coming down here."

I finished up my work early and gave Cindy a call. She was getting ready to head out to Hartford for her own family Christmas.

"How did the interview go?" she asked.

"I think it went well," I said. "I was so nervous this morning that I puked my brains out and skipped my run."

"When are you leaving for Long Island?"

"Tomorrow morning. We have a reservation on the ferry out of New London at one. Steven is coming down later today to help me pick out a Christmas present for his parents. Any suggestions?"

"A block of ice for his mother?" she said laughing. I laughed too.

"Thanks. I needed that."

At around four, Steven appeared at my office door with an overnight bag. I got up from my desk and met him at the door. He smiled at me and leaned down to kiss me hello.

"Did you get your run in?" he asked.

"No, but I could try later." I said.

"Not if I have anything to do with it," he said playing moving his hands down my back to my backside.

"You really are too much. I thought we were going shopping for a gift for your parents?" I asked.

"That won't take too long," he said. "Besides what my mother really needs you can't give her."

"What's that?" I asked intrigued.

"A swift kick in the ass!" he said laughing. I smiled. "Good. I made you laugh. I was thinking of a nice bottle of wine and some New England trinkets."

"Did you eat dinner?" I asked.

"No. What do you want to eat?" he asked.

"I'm in the mood for some Chinese food. There's a great place around the corner," I said. I grabbed my purse. "We'll stop back here before we go back to my place."

"Promise," he said hitting my butt.

"Calm down," I warned. "Were you this horny with Chelsea?"

"No. I've never been this horny. I don't know what it is you do to me," he said. "While Chelsea and I were dating, I was working my ass off at NYU. I was too tired most days to do anything but sleep. I think I've made love to you more in the last month than Chelsea and I made love the whole time we were dating."

His statement shocked me. We left my office and headed out to dinner. After dinner Steven picked out nice basket, a few bottles of wine, and a few knickknacks from a local antique store. We made our way back to the hospital and picked up our bags. Steven insisted on grabbing a cab back to my apartment.

We settled on the couch to watch a movie. I had spent some time on the Internet getting Steven his Christmas present. I had found two sets of bookends for his office at home. One was medically inspired and the other was nautical. At the end of the movie, he surprised me with a small box jewelry box. I opened the box to find a beautiful pair of amethyst earnings.

"Steven," I breathed. "They're beautiful. Where did you get them?" In the box was a designer's name.

"I found the designer online. She makes jewelry with meaning behind them. The gold is for childhood cancer and the amethyst is for Hodgkin's disease."

I was stunned. He pulled out another box. This one was long and flat. I opened it to find the matching necklace.

"Tomorrow," he said, "I'll put this necklace on you. I want to open the clasp myself." He leaned forward and kissed my neck.

"I don't know what to say." I didn't have anything as nice as this to give him. "I'm afraid my gifts for you are boring in comparison." I went over to the small Christmas tree in my apartment and took out the boxes.

He opened the boxes to find the bookends. "They're perfect," he said with a smile. "I've finally contacted a company about putting bookshelves into my office. Thank you." He leaned down and kissed me again.

I smiled. I had no idea he had done that. I was very pleased with myself. "What should I pack for the stay at your parents' house?"

"We're cooking dinner tomorrow night for my parents. So casual for Christmas Eve. Dinner Christmas Day is always at Shinnicock. That would mean dressier. As for meeting Tommy and his wife Julie, jeans are fine. And a bathing suit."

"A bathing suit?" I asked.

"For the hot tub," he said. "My parents have a great hot tub outside. There's something really decadent about sitting out in the hot tub while it's snowing."

I was stunned. "OK. I'll pack a bathing suit. Can you help me with the outfit for Christmas Day?"

"Fine. Go into your room and pick out a few outfits, try them on for me, and I'll let you know what works."

I went into my room and went through the closet. I picked out a few dresses I had. There was the little black dress, an emerald green suit, and a navy sheath dress. I put on the green suit first. I came out and he whistled.

"Nice, but a little too business for dinner," He commented. I could tell he was enjoying this. I changed into the navy dress.

"Much better," he said. "By the way are you going to model the swim suits for me?"

"No!" I called from the bedroom. I put on my little black dress. I was planning to wear that to the rehearsal dinner for Judy's wedding. I came out into the living room.

"Wow!" he whistled. I stopped in front of him and turned. "Wow."

"I was planning to wear it to the rehearsal dinner for Judy's wedding." I explained.

"What?" he sputtered. "I'm sorry, I was distracted for a minute."

I laughed. "I said I was going to wear this to the rehearsal dinner for Judy's wedding. Is it too much for Christmas dinner?"

"No, but it's too distracting. The navy one is your best bet. Come here. There's a string hanging from your dress."

"Where?" I said coming over to him. I had picked up the hem of the skirt when he pulled me down onto his lap. I realized that the string was just a ploy to get me within arms' reach of him. "You're bad." I said as he began to put his hand up my dress.

"I can't wait until tomorrow when I have my left hand back," he murmured next to my neck.

I laughed. "I doubt if I'll be able to handle you with two good hands." His right hand had made its way between my thighs. I sighed.

"Handle is exactly what I have in mind for tomorrow." He said as he began to pull my panties down. "My God you have the best legs." He put his hands beneath my knees and stood up with me in his arms. He walked into my bedroom and put me down next to my bed. I unzipped my dress and let it fall to the floor. I quickly took off my bra and dove into bed.

Steven took off his clothes and joined me in bed. As he leaned over me, I stared into his eyes. He took his finger and traced the outline of my lips. I kissed his fingertip. He moved his finger down my chin and throat. I closed my eyes at the sensual moment. He traced the line down my throat in between my breasts.

"Steven," I said in a whisper.

"Hmm," he answered as he moved to my right breast. That one finger was trailing across my nipple and it reacted.

"Can I ask you a question?" I said. I had to concentrate. It was taking all I could to concentrate.

"Yeah," he said trailing that finger to my left breast.

"Tell me." I began but couldn't continue as his finger moved down to my bellybutton and began to trace it.

"I love you." He said tracing the scar from my radiation treatments.

"No," I said trying to correct his assumption.

"Yes?" He said moving the finger down my left thigh.

I shook my head. He moved his finger back up my right thigh. He gently pushed my thighs apart and moved his finger through the pubic hair. Slowly he eased the finger inside me. I groaned. He kissed my lips and captured the groan. He rolled over me and leaned on his forearms. I could feel him push inside me. I arched up and he groaned.

I lifted my legs to wrap them around him as he began to move inside me. He captured my left leg and hooked it with his arm. He guided it up until my heel was on his shoulder. The whole time he caressed my leg and continued to push inside me. He followed by treating my right leg to the same treatment. His movements increased as he continued to push deeply inside me. I began to lose all control as he became more insistent. He reached between us and with the one finger that started it all brought me to a climax that tore a scream from my throat.

I don't remember him putting my legs down. He rested his forehead on my forehead. Gently he kissed my lips and rolled to his back pulling me onto his chest. The cold cast on his left arm made me gasp.

"I can't wait until tomorrow. Nine a.m. can't come soon enough," he said stroking my back. "What is you wanted me to tell you?"

I paused trying to remember. "How many women have there been?" I finally asked.

"Why does it matter?" he asked as his right hand caressing my spine.

"I want to know," I said. "I told you my sordid past."

"You're not old enough to have a sordid past. Patrick's dominatrix doesn't count." He was avoiding my question.

I rolled over and put my back to him. He realized my anger and pulled me into him.

"I'm sorry," he said. "I'm not trying to avoid the question." He paused. "OK, I am. I'm not proud of the number of women I've slept with. I couldn't even give you an accurate number."

I held my breath for a moment.

"Most of the women I've slept with are from the club. Some of them wanted me. Some of them wanted my mother's money. Some of them were trying to get back at their parents. I can't explain it. But I want you to understand something." He rolled me over and looked into my eyes. "I know the difference. I'm thirty years old and I've been sleeping with women since I was fifteen. You are definitely the real deal. There's no comparison."

I began to well up with tears. Again.

"No more crying," he warned as he wiped the tears away. "You need some sleep. I want you well rested for tomorrow. I want to run my hands all over you." He held up his left hand to remind me again that he was getting his cast removed. I smiled at him and closed my eyes to go to sleep.

"I love you," he whispered in my ear.

"I love you too," I answered yawning.

Chapter Twenty-Six

♥

I heard the alarm go off at seven and Diana was out of bed immediately. I didn't think anything of her rushing out of bed until I heard the sound of her retching in the bathroom. I groggily rolled out of bed and wandered to the bathroom door.

"Diana?" I called as I knocked. "Are you OK?"

"Yeah," she answered. She opened the door and came out into the living room. Her face was pale and her forehead was covered with sweat.

"Get back in bed now." I said.

"I was planning on it." She said. "I'm so tired this morning. I slept hard last night. I don't even remember dreaming."

"How long have you felt like this?" I asked.

"It started yesterday," she said. "I think it's just nerves." She said with a weak smile.

"What's to be nervous about?" I asked

"Oh I don't know," she said sarcastically with her arms folded across her chest. "I'm trying to get a new job and going to your parents' house for the first time. All in the same week."

"Get back in bed," I instructed feeling her head for a fever. "Doctor's orders."

She laughed and walked back to the bedroom. She did lie down in bed. I sat next to her brushing the hair off her face.

She smiled at me and closed her eyes. "Probably one of the many times I'll be thankful you are a doctor."

"Trust me. It can be a pain in the ass," I said. "Especially when you get hit by cars and a bossy public relations officer won't let you sign yourself out AMA." I leaned down to kiss her forehead. She smiled weakly.

I jumped in the shower and began to think about all the things that could be wrong with her. She could be right and it could be nerves. My mother was definitely not the warmest spot in anyone's life. I'm sure Diana wasn't the first woman to be ill at the prospect of spending time with my mother. I hoped it was nerves and not something more. I had read enough about Hodgkin's to know that it could be a reoccurrence of the disease. That was the worst-case scenario.

I walked out of the bathroom freshly showered. In her bedroom, I noticed she was asleep again. I sat down on the bed and put on a pair of jeans and a sweater. I pushed back the hair from her face. I leaned down and kissed her lips lightly. She smiled in her sleep. I grabbed my car keys pausing to leave her a note on the counter. I headed out to the T with the plan to pick up my car at the hospital and drive back to her apartment.

At the hospital, everything went as planned. The cast came off and the doctor gave me a brace to wear. Out of respect for my patients, he was able to cut the cast off with as little damage to it as possible. As a pediatrician, most of my patients over the last month had pestered me to sign my cast. I very proudly carried my cast to my car and began the drive back to Diana's apartment.

I parked the car on the street and made my way up to the apartment. When I knocked at the door, she answered in her bathrobe. I held up my now free left hand. She laughed.

"You're worse than your patients," she said. She turned back to the bedroom and began getting dressed in a short black skirt with a v-neck plum sweater. I remembered my promise to her and grabbed the back box with the amethyst necklace. I opened it and unclasped the necklace. I went up behind her as she was doing her makeup and put it around her neck. Her hair had been pulled up in a twist. I bent down to kiss her neck as I finished.

"Thanks," she said.

"You're feeling better?" I asked.

She nodded. "Still a little tired, but not sick."

"When was your last check up?" I asked. "You still go once year to get a clean bill of health."

She turned and looked at me. "I have an appointment scheduled for next month. Please don't worry. It's not the Hodgkin's again."

"Fine," I said. "I won't worry, but I want a promise. If you're still not feeling well after you hear about the job, you move your appointment up."

"Promise," she said. She turned around and grabbed her bags. "What time is our ferry?"

"One." I said. It was around ten. "If we leave now, we may make the noon ferry or we could pick up the stuff we need for dinner in New London."

"OK," she said. "Can I sleep in the car some more?"

"You can do anything you want to do in the car." I said cupping her face with both my hands. I kissed her gently and took her bags and the small overnight bag I had brought to her house last night. She grabbed her purse and the gift basket.

We settled ourselves into the car for the approximately two-hour drive to New London. She was asleep by the time we were on Interstate 495 South. Her skirt had ridden up while she was sleeping and her legs were leaning toward me. I found myself tempted to caress her leg. By the time we were on I95, I gave into the temptation of putting my hand on her leg. She had on sheer stockings that added to the silkiness of her skin. I had never really been a legman, but my God, she had gorgeous legs.

Before I knew it, I had pushed her skirt up higher with my caresses. In Rhode Island, there was a sign for a rest stop just before the Connecticut border. I remembered it from Labor Day weekend. I was desperate to use the bathroom and was surprised to find that this particular rest stop didn't have one. Not only that, it was secluded in the woods. I saw the sign and smiled. I exited 195 and pulled into the secluded rest stop. When the car came to a stop, she woke up.

"Are we here already?" Diana asked as she stretched.

"No," I answered. "I needed to stop." I unbuckled my seatbelt.

"Are you OK?" she asked. "I hope this puking thing isn't a virus."

"No," I said leaning over to kiss her and unbuckle her seatbelt. "I just remembered what I loved the most about having two good arms."

"What's that?" she asked innocently.

"I can actually caress your leg while I drive a car," I said putting both of my hands on her knees and running them up her legs. "Or I can stop at a rest stop and run both my hands up your legs at the same time."

"Do we really have time?" she asked finally realizing where I wanted things to go.

"Do I really care?" I said. I pushed my seat back as far as it would go and began to unbuckle my pants.

She pulled her skirt up and pulled off her pantyhose and underwear. She climbed over the emergency break and stick shift between the two front seats. I pulled her down hard on top of me. There wasn't much room for her legs to move. In the position she was in, I began thrusting upward into her. Her hips were moving as much as they could. There was an awkward moment when she leaned back and sounded the horn.

We laughed and I pulled her forward to kiss her. I was crazed. I began thrusting wildly inside her. She was so tight. I grabbed her hips and slammed into her. She collapsed on top of me and I pulled her down for a kiss.

"I don't think I'll ever pass this rest stop again without smiling," I said. I checked the time. It was a little before noon. We were too late for the noon ferry but would be early for the ferry at one.

"We're going to just miss the noon ferry," I said.

"It was worth it," she said laughing. "Can we stop at a store to get the things we need for dinner as well as a new pair of pantyhose? I know I ripped them to shreds while trying to get them off." She eased off me and slid back into the passenger seat.

I groaned. It took me a minute to pull up my boxers and pants.

"We're not going to run into any of your old flames while we're in town, are we?" she questioned me.

"No," I said. "There really aren't any old flames. Just a bunch of now married debutants who wanted to have fun."

"What about Chelsea?" she asked as she pulled her skirt down and buckled into her seat.

I laughed. "Chelsea is in Pennsylvania visiting her finace's parents. She's the only girlfriend of mine that I actually want you to meet. She's not from the country club set. My best friend Tommy is her brother. She would give you the best tips on how to deal with my mother."

"What can *you* tell me to deal with your mother?"

"There are two lines of defense against my mother. The first is my father and the second is me. Right now you have me and I have my dad." I explained.

We were in New London before we knew it. We stopped at a local Stop and Shop to pick up the necessary ingredients for dinner. We purchased a cooler bag as well to keep the fish fresh for the next three hours. We arrived at the ferry with about half an hour to spare. I drove the car onto the ferry and then we went up into the passenger area to have lunch.

"How's the stomach?" I asked.

"Better," she sighed. "I'm still really nervous. I don't want to cause problems between you and your mom."

I laughed. "You won't cause problems. The problems between us have been there for a long time. She's really not a bad person. She just loves to keep me in line. It's her way of paying back my dad."

"What do you mean?" she asked.

"Let's just put it this way, my mother has a lot of baggage that she hasn't gotten rid of. I keep trying to get her to let go. I'm not sure if she will. If you just keep that in mind, she won't seem so bad."

She looked at me puzzled.

"Diana," I asked, "do you trust me?"

She nodded.

"Do you love me?" I asked.

She looked down and nodded again.

"That's all that matters," I reiterated. "Come outside with me. I want some fresh air." I pulled her outside and into my arms. I loved the fresh sea air. It was cold out but I was happy to be outside.

"How's the arm?" she asked.

"Great. I can't wait to sit in the hot tub tonight and get my whole arm wet. Did you pack your swim suit?"

"Yes," she said with a sigh. "When we get to your parents' house, do I have my own room?"

"Of course," I said, "but if you think I'm not sneaking into your room nightly you're living in a dream world."

"Please don't get me in trouble with your parents," she begged.

"I promise," I said. The shoreline was looming in the distance. "We're almost there. Let's go back to the car." I took her hand and led her back to the car and we settled in. I looked over at her and her face was pale again.

"Are you OK?" I asked. I put my hand up to her forehead. It was clammy. I reached over and reclined her seat. "Breathe for me." I put my hand on her wrist and took her pulse. It was rapid.

"Diana," I said her name. She turned her head toward me and smiled weakly. "Take deep breaths. Close your eyes." I was checking her pulse again and pushing the hair away from her face.

The ferry docked and I made my way off the boat onto the shore. It was another half hour to forty-five minutes until we reached my parents' house. Diana slept most of the way. As I pulled onto the long beach road leading up to my parents' house, I reached over to wake her up.

"Diana," I whispered. "Diana, we're almost there."

Her eyes opened and slowly she sat up.

"Sorry about that," she said.

"It's OK," I said but I was worried about her. There had been too many incidents too close together to be just nerves. "Here's the house."

I turned in the driveway and watched her eyes widen at the sight of the sprawling house and grounds. I then watched her face grow pale and she began to tug at her skirt. She looked over at me, panic in her eyes.

"It's just a house," I said trying to console her.

Chapter Twenty-Seven

♥

I didn't understand what was going on with me. I was very nervous about spending the holiday with Steven's parents. I wanted them to like me. I wanted things to be relaxed. Between applying for the job and the stress of spending the holiday at his parents' house, I had made myself sick. He was so patient with me on the ride to the house. I couldn't believe how tired I was. I knew he was worried. I was worried. I promised him I would go see a doctor. Working in a hospital, that was an easy promise to keep. I would have them run a series of tests. I knew what they would be looking for and I hoped they wouldn't find it.

When Steven woke me up, I felt better until I saw his parents' house. It was a huge house on the water. I must have looked frightened because Steven turned to me and calmly said, "It's just a house."

Steven parked his car outside the garage. I grabbed my bag to carry in. Steven immediately took it from me. Instead he handed me the gift basket for his parents. We walked to the front door. Steven rang the doorbell and his father answered it.

"Hey," he said hugging Steven. "You made good time." We walked into the house.

"Monica," he called, "Steven and Diana are here." He turned to me. "It's good to see you again Diana." He kissed my cheek hello.

"Thank you for having me, Dr. Edwards." I said.

"Please call me Kevin."

I was busy taking in the enormous living room that I was standing in. The floor was all hardwood. There was an enormous stone fireplace on one wall. The wall opposite the door was all windows with a spectacular view of the water. There was a sweeping double stairway that led to the second floor. Steven's mom entered the room from those stairs. She was dressed in a pair of black wool slacks with a royal blue silk shirt. She was so stunningly beautiful even in her fifties that it was easy to see where Steven inherited his good looks.

"Really Kevin. There's no need to shout," she scolded walking down the stairs.

She crossed the living room to Steven and me. She came and kissed him on the cheek and shook my hand politely. "How nice of you to come."

"Thank you for having me Mrs. Edwards," I said. "Steven helped me put together this basket for you. Merry Christmas."

"Thank you," she said taking the basket. She placed it on a side table in the living room without really looking at it.

"Steven. Why don't you show Diana to the blue room?" Mrs. Edwards said to him.

"Sure mom," Steven said. I followed him up the stairs down the hallway. "My mom likes to call the rooms by the different colors they've been decorated in. I haven't quite figured out why she does that."

He opened the door to the bedroom to bring me inside. It was definitely blue. The room was all shades of blue ranging from navy to light blue. It was very beautiful. There was a queen-size brass bed with a blue striped comforter. There was a wall of windows including French doors that led to a balcony. The view from the windows was breathtaking. I went to stand in front of the windows. Steven came up behind me and wrapped his arms around me.

"Can you see my sailboat?" he said pointing to the boat that was up out of the water. "I can't wait to sail her up to Boston. I need to find someplace to keep her in the Boston area. You don't know any place off hand?"

I shook my head. I was afraid to speak. I was overwhelmed by the sheer wealth that surrounded me. I didn't speak because I was sure I would begin to cry.

"My room's next door. I actually share the balcony with you," he said next to my ear. "Do you want to come downstairs with me? I'm anxious to start dinner."

"Sure," was all I was able to get out, "I just want to freshen up."

He turned me around and looked down at me. "Are you feeling all right?"

I nodded my head.

"A little overwhelmed?" he asked.

I nodded my head again.

"Can I ask you to remember something?"

I nodded.

"It's not my house. It's not my money. It's my parents."

I nodded again.

"One more thing," he said tilting my head up so that I was forced to look into his deep blue eyes. "I love you." He leaned down to kiss me. "I'm giving you ten minutes and then I'm sending my mother up to get you."

I groaned. He laughed and left the room. As soon as he left, I began to cry silently. I pulled out my phone. I dialed Cindy's cell. I didn't know who else to call.

"Hey babe," Cindy answered. "What's up?"

"I'm in my room at his parents' house," I sniffed. "Oh Cindy. I'm so out of my element here."

"Calm down," she said. "Take a picture and send it to me."

I did what she asked and she reacted. "Wow. Remind me not to invite him to my father's beach house in Niantic."

"You're not helping," I said to her. "What am I going to do?"

"Suck it up," Cindy advised. "Who cares how much money he has? Does he love you?"

"Yes," I said quietly.

"Do you love him?" she asked.

"Yes," I said again.

"What's going on with you?" she asked. "I can't believe I am talking to the same woman who scanned S and M pictures of her ex-boyfriend into her computer as an insurance policy. Aren't you the same woman who deals with obnoxious press as well as obnoxious Kennedy cousins?"

"Whatever," I said. "I'm nervous. I'm so nervous I've made myself sick."

"What do you mean?" Cindy asked.

"I vomited yesterday morning and this morning. I almost passed out on the ferry. I'm really tired," I said.

"If I didn't know you better, I'd say you were pregnant," Cindy said. "But since that's not possible, you're worried it's the cancer again?"

"Yes," I said. "It wasn't like this when I was thirteen, but there are similar symptoms."

"Go see the doctor when you get back from Long Island."

"I know," I said with a sigh. "I've got to go. Any advice?"

"Have a great big glass of wine, relax, and be yourself." Cindy continued, "And..."

"And what?" I asked.

"Fuck his brains out." Cindy said with a chortle.

"Thanks for the advice, but I did that at a rest stop on the way down." I said.

I silenced her laughing when I pressed 'end' on the cell phone. I checked my makeup in the mirror and sighed. I opened the bedroom door and began to walk down the hallway. I walked down the staircase into the living room. I could hear the clank of the pots and pans in the kitchen. I followed the sounds.

"YOU learned to cook?" I heard his father say.

"Yes. Thank you. Diana taught me a couple of really great dishes," Steven boasted.

"How provincial," his mother said.

"Mother!" Steven warned.

I walked in the room and the conversation ended. "Sorry. Cindy called."

"No problem. Are you going to redeem me?" he asked.

"They don't believe I can really cook."

"He did an excellent job," I said. I went to stand with him as he began combining the ingredients. "He's a quick learner."

"He's always been very smart," his mother bragged. "He was top ten in high school, college, and medical school."

"Mother," Steven warned again. "Diana doesn't need to know my class ranks or GPA." He turned to me. "Can you help me with the salad? You do that so much better than I do."

I nodded happy to be doing something.

"Diana," Kevin Edwards said, "Steven said you're a bridesmaid in a wedding on New Year's Eve."

"Yes. My college roommate Judy is getting married in Chicago on New Year's Eve. It's black tie optional."

"Hey mom," Steven said, "you were right to make me buy that tux. I finally get to wear it."

Monica Edwards sighed and poured another glass of wine.

"Mothers always know best," I said trying to get on her good side. "Steven's been teaching me to dance as well."

"Really?" she said. "Isn't that nice of you."

Dinner was almost ready. Steven served it in the dining room. We sat down to eat.

"What mass are we going to tomorrow morning?" Kevin Edwards asked.

"How about eleven?" Mrs. Edwards suggested. "Is that too late Steven?" She glanced my way, "Or maybe too early?"

"Eleven's fine," he said. "Diana, are you going for a run tomorrow morning?"

"Normally I'd say no, but since I missed yesterday and today, I need to get a run in tomorrow."

"Why did you miss your run?" Mr. Edwards asked.

"I wasn't feeling well," I explained.

"I hope you're not coming down with something," Mrs. Edwards said.

"Probably not."

"Steven said you had cancer when you were a teenager," she continued, "no chance of that coming back?"

"Mother!" Steven pleaded, "Really!" He turned to me, "Sorry."

"No, really, it's OK." I said. "No Mrs. Edwards the chances of me coming out of remission are very small. I have a checkup every year to make sure. My annual check up is coming up."

"That had to be difficult having cancer as a teenager."

"It wasn't easy," I admitted. "I was very lucky. My treatments worked and I had a perfect bone marrow donor in my brother Jack."

"How lucky for you," Mrs. Edwards said. "You do work for the Leukemia and Lymphoma Society now?"

"Yes ma'am," I explained. "It helps when a patient can meet someone that has survived the treatments and the disease."

"What's the next event you're working on for them?" Steven asked.

"There's an art show the weekend after New Year's," I said. "I'm not in charge of that one, but it benefits the Team in Training for the Boston Marathon."

"An art show? Mom that's right up your alley." Steven repeated his statement from brunch at the Andover Inn. I could tell he was desperate to have his mother connect with me.

"My wife has an art degree from Vassar College," Kevin Edwards explained. "Maybe we'll come up and make a weekend out of it."

"We'll see," Mrs. Edwards said. "Do you have a dessert Steven?"

"No, we haven't really advanced that far in my cooking lessons," he apologized.

"Well it's a good thing that I have an apple pie," Mrs. Edwards practically snickered. She excused herself from the table and went to the kitchen and returned with a gourmet apple pie.

After dessert, Steven and I cleared the table and loaded the dishwasher. It was almost eight. Steven's parents excused themselves for the evening and went up to their room. Steven pulled me into his arms in the kitchen and kissed me.

"Thank you," he said.

"For what?" I asked.

"For not killing my mother," he said leaning down to kiss me. "For being you."

I smiled tersely at him.

"Do you want to check out the hot tub?" he asked. "We could polish off that bottle of wine and listen to the ocean. That would relax you."

"Sure," I said. We went upstairs to change. I put on my bikini with a pair of sweatpants and sweatshirt over it. I remembered what Steven had said about the balcony, and walked to his balcony door. I was about to go in when I heard his mother's voice.

"How do you know she's not using you?" she said. "She's Canadian. She probably needs a green card. And wouldn't you be an excellent candidate."

"Mother," Steven warned, "It's not like that."

"Sure it is," she said. "Can't you see it? She probably has no medical coverage from the cancer. She has the ridiculous job at the hospital and wouldn't marrying you be a great promotion for her? Next thing you know she'll tell you she's pregnant and expect you to marry her."

I turned around and walked back into my room. I sat heavily on the bed. So that's what she thought of me. I was a gold digger. I was looking for a free ride by marrying him. Oh my God. If I could have left the house at that very moment, I would have. To have someone say all those things about you was bad enough, to hear it was another layer of pain.

I didn't hear the door open. Suddenly Steven was standing in front of me. He was wearing a pair of swim trunks and a Fordham Sailing sweatshirt. I looked up at him. There must have been tears in my eyes.

"What's wrong?" he asked kneeling in front of me.

I shook my head. I couldn't tell him I overheard the conversation. It would make me look terrible; like I was everything that his mother said I was.

"What's wrong?" he asked more insistently.

"Nothing. I'm just tired," I said.

"You need to relax. Come on," he said pulling me up. "Doctor's orders. You need a good long soak in the hot tub."

He took my hand, led me out of the blue bedroom and downstairs. We walked through the family room with its built-in mahogany bookcases and wide fireplace to the garden room. It was a beautiful greenhouse that had a stone patio off to the side. On the stone patio was a ten-person hot tub. Steven went outside, uncovered it and turned it on. He came back in, grabbed towels from a cabinet inside, and pulled me outside.

"Now," he said pulling off his sweatshirt. "Take off those sweats and relax."

I stripped out of the sweatpants and sweatshirt and stepped out into the cold air. I stepped into the hot tub and sat down. Steven jumped in and pulled me in front of him. He began to massage my back and the back of my neck.

"You've got a lot going on right now," he said. "I'm sorry if I added to your stress." He leaned down and kissed my neck.

"It's OK," I said. "Tell me about your parents' house. I love old houses."

"Let's see. My grandfather bought it in the 1950s. It used to be part of a hotel he had stayed in. I don't even want to think what he paid for it-- something outrageously cheap. He used it as a summer home until he retired. When he retired, he moved out here full time." He was massaging my back while he talked. "There's an apartment above the boat house that I used to spend most of my time in when I was in high school and college. Now my parents rent it out to the summer help."

"Summer help?" I asked.

"My mom likes to have the nicest lawn in the neighborhood. She hires a gardener for the summer. It's usually some college kid. My grandfather used to do the same thing."

He turned me around to face him. "Feeling better?"

I nodded and put my head on his shoulder. He untied the string holding my bikini top in place. He took the top off and placed it on the side of the hot tub.

"I don't why I told you to pack the bathing suit; I knew I would just get you naked in here anyway." He began to pull at the bottoms.

"Have you ever…" I began to ask as he worked the bottoms off and placed them on the side with the top.

He shook his head no, "No. I've never done this in my parents hot tub." He pulled his swim trunks off. "I've never had the opportunity nor the inclination."

"So this is a first for you too," I said.

"Yes," he said parting my legs to straddle him. "I can't believe how perfect this night is. Did you notice it's a full moon?"

I shook my head no.

"It's trying to snow. I have the best Christmas present in the world," he said. "I have a goddess who loves me and she's naked in a hot tub with me." He entered me as I leaned down to kiss him. I gasped into his mouth.

"Steven," I whispered. I began to move with him in the swirling water. "Tell me what you want." It was his fantasy. I wanted to make it perfect for him.

"You," he said. "This is perfect. You're perfect." He was taking his time. He was kissing my neck and caressing my breasts. His tempo increased and I began to feel the beginnings of my orgasm.

"Do you love me?" he asked.

"Yes," I answered. "Do you love me?"

"Yes," he answered. "No matter what?"

"Yes!" I screamed as he pulsed inside me. I collapsed onto his shoulder. I was crying. I knew I loved him but at the same time I knew I didn't want to live with the cloud of suspicion his mother had cast over me.

"Diana," he said caressing my back. "I need to ask you something."

"Hmm," I was too afraid for words.

"What happens if you don't get this job?" he asked.

"I start all over again," I answered.

"What do you mean?" he asked.

"I have to look for a new job. They're getting rid of my position at the end of January. Phasing it out so to speak."

"And what about your visa?"

"I'd have to find someplace willing to hire me or I have to go home." I explained.

"You couldn't stay?" he asked.

"If I don't have the right paperwork, I'd be deported and wouldn't be able to come back into the US for any reason for five years."

He whistled, "That's tough."

"September 11th made everyone suspect," I said. I couldn't help but think of his mother's conversation with him in his room.

"What if you married me?" he asked. "Could you stay if you married me?"

I looked into his eyes and put my fingers on his lips. "I need to stay because I've earned it. I need to stay because I can make it. Not because you feel sorry for me. It's no way to start a life." I got off his lap and grabbed one of the towels.

"Diana," he called. I wrapped the towel around me and made my way back into the greenhouse. He was out of the hot tub and caught up to me in the greenhouse. The tears were streaming down my face.

"Diana," he said trying to pull me into his arms. I pulled away.

"Is that what you think of me?" I said to him. "That I want you to marry me so that I can stay in the US?"

"No," he said quietly. "I just wanted you to know that I don't want you to have to leave. I didn't mean to make you angry."

"Do you often ask women to marry you because you don't want them to leave?" I said. I could tell I hit a nerve. "Did you ask Chelsea to marry you when you moved to Boston?"

He looked down.

"Did you?" I asked angrily.

"Yes," he said quietly. "It was wrong. I was wrong to ask her. She said 'no.'"

"How do you know it's not wrong again?" I asked quietly. "I don't want a man to ask me to marry me because he feels sorry for me. I want a man to ask me to marry him because he can't live without me."

"Diana," he pleaded. "I'm sorry. I didn't mean to make you think I felt sorry for you. I just wanted you to know I want to be there for you if you need me."

"Thanks, but I need to make this work," I said. "I need to make it work by myself. It was my choice to move here. I have to make it work. If I can't, I need to leave."

I turned and left him standing there in the greenhouse. I made it back up to my room and fell onto the bed crying. I was crying for all the things I had lost. I had moved to Boston on a whim following what I thought was love. It fell apart and I was left putting everything back together again. Just when I had things under control, Steven walked into my life. He made me happy again. I knew I loved him. I just wasn't sure how he felt about me. I lost faith in him tonight. I heard Steven walk down the hallway. I could see his shadow pause at my door. I held my breath. I heard him take the last few steps into his room and close the door. I fell asleep exhausted. At one point, I thought I felt Steven's arms around me. I thought I heard his voice. I dreamt of him.

I woke up to find a red rose on my night table. Next to it was a card and a long flat box. I picked up the card and opened it. The outside said "Merry Christmas to the one I love." I opened the card to read what he had written.

Dear Diana,

I cannot tell you how happy I have been this past month. I know it is hard for you to understand how alone and unhappy I have been most of my life. I have had little to smile and laugh about. You have brought me that. I hope that I make you happy. I couldn't resist buying you one more piece of jewelry.

Merry Christmas.

I Love You,

Steven

I opened the box to find the matching bracelet for the necklace and earrings. It was breathtaking. I couldn't believe he had bought another piece of jewelry.

I looked at the clock. It was a little after eight. I felt OK. I got up and put on my running clothes. I had fallen asleep wrapped in the towel I had taken from the hot tub. At some point during the night I had ended up under the covers. I walked down the hall quietly and slipped out the front door. I ran down the long driveway to the road. I ran for about twenty minutes in one direction and then turned around to return. I passed some pretty magnificent houses. I couldn't believe what I saw. I returned to the house to find Steven's parents in the living room with coffee.

"Good morning," Kevin Edwards said as I walked in the front door. "Did you have a good run?"

"Yes," I said bending to untie my shoes. "There are some beautiful houses in your neighborhood."

"Yes there are," Mrs. Edwards said clipped. She rose from the couch and went into the kitchen.

"If you'll excuse me," I said walking to the stairs, "I'm going to get a shower in." I climbed the stairs and made it to my room. What I hadn't planned was to find Steven asleep in my bed.

I walked over to the bed. I sat down next to him and kissed his lips. He opened his eyes.

"I thought I was supposed to kiss sleeping beauty awake," he said.

"You are sleeping beauty." I said, "What are you doing in my bed?"

"I came in when I woke up but I guess I missed you," he said. "I figured the easiest way to apologize was to wait for you. I fell asleep waiting."

"Sorry," I said. "I was talking to your parents in the living room."

"I'm sorry," he said. "Can we forget last night?"

"No," I said. "Steven...."

He reached up and put his fingers across my lips. "I can't take it back. I can't change what happened, but I want you to give me a chance."

I shook my head.

"Why not?" he begged.

"I need some time," I said. "Give me some time."

"Am I still going to Chicago with you?" he asked. There was sadness in his eyes.

"If you still want to go, you can go, but I need some time alone after that. If I don't have a job after the wedding, I'll need to spend a lot of time finding a new job. Everything depends on the job."

He nodded. "What do you want to do today?"

"I don't want to ruin your Christmas. Let's go to mass and then dinner at the club. When were we supposed to meet up with Tommy?"

"Tomorrow," he said. "Do you want to try to do it tonight instead?"

"Sure," I said. "I need to get back to do some work as well as see a doctor. I need to get answers."

He nodded. "I'll call Tommy and see if we can do dessert with him at his parents' house and then head home from there."

"Thank you," I said.   "And thank you for the beautiful bracelet. It really was not necessary."

"I would give you the world if I could," he said getting up from bed. "I love you," he said leaving.

"I love you too," I whispered to the closed door.

Chapter Twenty-Eight

I couldn't understand how things went so badly so quickly. I hadn't meant to make Diana angry. I hadn't meant to hurt her, but I did. I wished I had never come home for Christmas. My mother always had a way of making life difficult for me.

We went to mass and from there to Shinnicock. Diana looked absolutely gorgeous in her navy blue dress. I was proud to have her with me. As we sat down for dinner, a few friends of my parents stopped by to say hello. Diana and I sat patiently as they spoke with them. I knew a few of them and would introduce Diana to them. She was polite but distant. After dinner was finished, there was dancing. Before I could excuse us to leave to meet up with Tommy, my father had stood and offered his hand to Diana.

"Diana," my father said, "would you dance with me?"

"I don't know," she said hesitantly, "I'm not too good."

"Nonsense," he said taking her hand and pulling her to the dance floor.

I looked over at my mother. She was watching them on the dance floor.

"Diana's angry with me," I said.

"Why?" She said looking at me.

"Last night I asked her what would happen if she didn't get the new job she applied for. In short, she said she could get deported. So I asked her if she could stay if I married her."

"You did what?" my mother hissed.

"She got angry with me. She told me she needed to do it on her own. She asked me if that was what I thought of her. I said no. I should have told her that's what you think of her."

"Steven!" she warned me.

"I'm sorry mother but I'm not backing down on this one," I said. "I love her. She makes me happy. She makes me laugh. Doesn't that mean something?"

She looked down at her plate.

"She's so worried about things, she's made herself sick. We're going home early tomorrow so that she can see a doctor." I said looking at her dancing with my father. "If it's the cancer again, I don't know what I would do. She said she wants a man who can't live without her. I can't live without her. I...."

"And if you had to choose between us and her?" she asked.

"If you make me choose, I would choose her," I said. "I would follow my heart. I never thought you would be so much like your mother. But I'll tell you one thing, I won't make the choice you made."

I got up from the table and cut in on my father.

"How are you feeling?" I asked Diana.

"Fine," she said with a weak smile. "Your dad is so nice."

"He is isn't he?" I said looking at my father. He had reached my mother. "He taught me everything he knows."

"He's arguing with your mom," she said. "What did you say to your mother?"

"I told her I couldn't live without you. I told her you made me happy. I told her you were the first person to make me laugh. I told her I loved you and that if I had to choose between my parents and you I would follow my heart."

"Steven," she gasped. "Don't do this. I told you I need time."

"Take all the time you want. I'm sure and I'll wait!" I said leading her off the dance floor. We were back at the table.

"Diana and I have to go," I said. "I promised Tommy Michaels we'd stop by his parents' house. We'll be home late and then up early to get back to Boston."

"Thank you for a wonderful time." Diana said.

"You're sweet," my father told her, "You come back to visit again. We'll come up for your art auction." He leaned over and kissed her cheek. He whispered something in her ear. She smiled at him.

My mother remained in her seat and wouldn't look at us. I leaned down to kiss her cheek. "Goodbye mother."

We left the club and headed to the Michaels' house in Hicksville. It was about a forty-five minute ride. Diana was watching me as I drove. I turned to her and she turned to stare out the window avoiding eye-contact.

"Diana," I said, "I told you my mother is my problem. Not yours. I'm solving my problem. This is the only way to solve the problem of my mother. You force her to make a decision."

She nodded her head. "I don't want to come between you and your parents."

"The problems between me and my parents are not because of you. We've had problems for a long time. In fact, you may solve many of our problems."

She nodded her head again. We arrived at Tommy's parents house around seven. I was happy to have other people around. I had never felt that way with Diana. Mrs. Michaels opened the front door.

"Steven," she said and embraced me with a hug and a kiss. "How was the drive?"

"Quiet," I said. "This is Diana Goyeau."

"Pleased to meet you," Mrs. Michaels said shaking Diana's hand. "Come in out of the cold. Tommy, Steven's here."

Tommy came out of the kitchen. "Hey. You made it," he said hugging me. "Merry Christmas. Did you bring your goddess?"

I smiled and gestured toward Diana. She seemed smaller than she really was next to Tommy's large size. Tommy walked toward her and picked her up in a bear hug.

"You have to be something special to make this one smile," he said kissing her check. "I've known him over ten years and I don't think I've ever seen his smile so wide."

"You have to be Tommy," Diana said to him with a smile.

"Heard about me have you?" he said to her. He turned to look at me. "What did you tell her about me?"

"Nothing that wasn't true," I said. "Where's Julie?"

"Putting the kids down. She'll be down in a minute."

"Sit down," Mrs. Michaels welcomed.

We sat down in the living room. I pulled Diana to sit next to me on the couch. She was still stiff. I leaned to whisper into her ear. "Relax. Steven's parents are easier than my parents."

"So Diana," Mrs. Michaels said. "Tommy said you're from Canada."

"Yes," she said curtly.

"She's spent the last twenty-four hours with my mother Mrs. Michaels," I said. "She needs to decompress."

Diana gasped, "Steven!"

Everyone else in the room laughed. Julie Michaels walked into the room.

"What's all the laughing about?" Julie asked.

"Steven's mom," Tommy offered.

Julie rolled her eyes and walked over to Diana. "You must be Diana." She bent her head to kiss her hello. "I'm Julie, Tommy's wife."

"Nice to meet you," Diana said.

"How are you Julie?" I said to her.

"Good Steven," she said. "How have you been?"

"Fantastic." I said smiling.

Tommy laughed. "You are too much. Diana, do you have any idea what he was like before you?"

Diana shook her head.

Julie explained, "Steven was an angry, suspicious man. You could get him to laugh every once in a while but he was so serious. Do you know the typical brooding young artist?"

Diana nodded.

"Steven was the brooding young doctor," Tommy said laughing.

Diana turned to look at me with a frown. She was checking my reaction to them. I held my hands up and said, "It's the truth. I'm the first to admit it. I had a real anger problem."

Again the room broke into laughter. Even Diana began to laugh this time. Julie pulled me up from the couch. "Come help me get the dessert."

I walked into the kitchen with Julie. She had a tray of cookies on the table.

"How bad was the visit with your parents?" Julie asked.

"Bad," I said. "She's been sick with nerves."

"What do you mean sick?" Julie asked with a frown.

"She's vomited a couple of times this week, she's really tired, and almost passed out on the ferry from New London," I said. "That's why we're here tonight. We're going home tomorrow so that she can see a doctor. I'm worried she's out of remission."

"Not to be doubting a doctor, but Steven, use your brain," Julie said.

"What do you mean use my brain?"

"Is she pregnant?" Julie asked.

"I doubt it," I said, "She was told that she can't have children from all the treatment she had as a teenager."

Julie started laughing. "Please tell me you haven't been banking on that as birth control."

"No," I said blushing, "We've used birth control."

"Every time?" Julie persisted.

"I think there were one or two times we didn't use birth control."

"By the time you leave tonight," Julie said, "I'll give you my professional opinion."

"And what profession would that be?"

"Mother." She said laughing as she walked out with the coffee pot.

Diana was looking more relaxed when we came back into the room. She was sitting on the couch with Tommy looking at a photo album.

"They weren't lying," she said. "I haven't seen a picture of you yet where you're smiling."

We spent the rest of the evening looking at old pictures and laughing. Julie asked Diana about her work with the Leukemia and Lymphoma Society.

"Her next big thing is an art auction," I said. "My parents may come up for it."

"Why would you torture her like that?" Julie pondered.

"We'll see if they really come up." I said. "Did you tell him about the wedding?"

"What wedding?" Julie snapped to attention.

"I'm a bridesmaid in a wedding in Chicago on New Year's Eve. Steven's coming with me. He taught me to dance for it."

"Excellent!" Julie said. "What did he teach you?"

"Salsa," Diana said. "We haven't danced since he had his cast off."

"Dance for us," Julie pleaded. Julie turned on the radio and found a Latin station.

I pulled Diana up and began dancing with her. She was as good as ever. It was as heated as ever by the time the dance was halfway over. After I had spun her numerous times, her face went pale. She broke away from me and ran toward the bathroom.

I followed her. I could hear her retching in the toilet. "Diana," I said softly at the door.

"Give me a minute," she whimpered. I heard the toilet flush and she came out. She was pale and clammy.

"I think we should go," I said to her. "You need to rest."

"OK," she said looking down. "I'm so embarrassed."

"Don't be," I said. "You were wonderful. You *are* wonderful."

We rejoined everyone in the living room. Julie had a big smile on her face. I excused us as we prepared to leave. Tommy and his parents hugged us goodbye. Julie hugged me and whispered in my ear, "Merry Christmas Papa."

I refused to believe she was right. I wanted to believe her, but that's the type of thing Julie or Tommy would say just to tease me. It was also something Diana would tell me. Diana fell asleep on the drive home. I woke her up and guided her inside my parents' home. I put her into her bed, stripped out of my clothes, and climbed into bed beside her. I caressed her stomach and wondered. I held her in my arms as I fell asleep.

Chapter Twenty-Nine

♥

I woke up to find Steven asleep beside me. I didn't have any clothes on. While I was watching him sleep, he woke up. He smiled at me. I brushed the hair from his forehead.

"Why are you in bed with me?" I asked.

"I was worried about you," he answered. "I undressed you and put you into bed."

"Thanks," I said. "I'm OK now." I was feeling OK but wanted to begin the process of getting home as soon as possible. If we left soon, I could stop at the hospital and schedule some appointments.

"You feel all right?" he asked pushing my hair off my face.

"I'm fine," I said. "Really."

He frowned at me. "You'd tell me if there was something wrong?"

"Of course," I said frowning back at him. "Can we get going soon? I'd love make a few appointments."

"Of course," he mimicked. "Have I told you today that I love you?"

I shook my head.

"I love you," he said kissing me. "No matter what." He got up out of bed and gathered up his clothes. He left.

I stretched and began to get ready. I had packed up most of my things on Christmas Day. I wasn't sure if the visit had gone completely horribly. I had had fun last night with Tommy and his family. Steven had invited them up for a visit. They were thinking of Martin Luther King Weekend. I would either be settled in my new job or searching for a new one.

The drive home was quiet. Steven dropped me off at my apartment. I called Cindy. She came over for the full story. I recounted the story of Steven's mother and the argument Steven had with her followed by the hot tub. I told her about the dancing at Tommy's house. She frowned.

"What's wrong?" I asked.

"Di," she said, "did you ever have unprotected sex with Steven?"

I thought. "Thanksgiving weekend at his house," I said. "Why do you ask?"

"I think you're pregnant," Cindy said. "Have you had your period since then?"

I thought. "No, but I'm never regular."

"I think you should take a pregnancy test."

"I can't be pregnant," I said.

"Can't meaning it's not possible? Or 'can't' in that you're scared?"

I started to cry. "Can't because she would think I planned it! Oh my God. I never thought I'd say it but I wish it was the cancer again."

"Don't say that!" Cindy said. "Listen. I'll go to the store and get a test."

She left me and I began to think about what she said. I began to think about what Steven's mother said. I was still staring into space when Cindy returned.

"Are you ready?" Cindy asked.

"No, but does it really matter?" I took the test into the bathroom and followed the instructions. I came out and set the timer. Cindy sat with me. The timer went off. I didn't move.

"Are you going to look?" Cindy asked.

"Can you do it for me?" I begged her. Cindy nodded. She walked into the bathroom and came back out holding the slim test stick.

"Didn't you tell me Steven said to not count on doctors?" Cindy said.

I nodded. "He said they practice medicine. They don't always get it right."

Cindy handed me the test. "And I'll tell you that you should play the lottery. You've been given two miracles in one life."

I looked down at it. I was pregnant. "Oh my God! Oh my God!" I began to cry. She sat down with me and pulled me into her arms.

"What am I going to do?" I cried. "What am I going to do?"

"Shh," Cindy said rocking me like the baby I was going to have. "Shh."

I was beginning to panic. "I don't know if I have a job. If I tell him, he'll think I planned it. Oh my God."

"Listen to me," Cindy said. "You need to tell him."

I nodded.

"I guess this means I'm running the marathon alone," Cindy said.

"I guess so," I laughed. "I'll be five months pregnant by then."

"There you go," she said. "Think positive."

I went to bed that night and slept fitfully. I woke up and went to work. The first order of business at work was to make an appointment to get my pregnancy confirmed. The second order of business was a noon appointment about my job or lack of it.

At noon, after I had vomited what little I had in my stomach, I reported to the Chief of Staff's office. I walked into his office and closed the door. There was a TV in his office.

"Good Morning Diana," he said.

"Good morning sir," I said. I was nauseous again.

"I was reviewing the footage from the press conferences you gave after Mr. Roberts was hit," he said. "I want you to know that I am very impressed with you."

That wasn't a good sign. Usually a statement like that was followed by a *but*. I was tensed waiting for the *but*.

"You really are a natural for the position," he said.

Again, not a great statement, "Thank you sir." I said.

"That's why we're offering you the position," he said.

Breathe. I told myself. Breathe. "Thank you sir." I repeated unable to come up with anything original.

He began to talk about the particulars. He began to explain the benefits. He was well aware of my visa issues and would have the paperwork taken care of by the hospital's attorneys. "I know you have a wedding on New Year's Eve in Chicago. Is it possible for you to be at work on January second?"

"I'll have to change my flight, but yes, I can be back for work on the second," I said.

He stood up. "Thank you Diana. Michelle is meeting with me next. Please try to be graceful as you leave. You know how she can be."

"No problem sir," I said. I shook his hand and walked out of his office. Michelle was waiting with a smug smile on her face. She obviously thought she had the position. I walked down to my office and thought about who I should call. I wanted to call Steven desperately, but I was afraid to tell him about being pregnant. I couldn't get an appointment until after the wedding. There was no sense in bringing it up until I was sure.

I called Steven at home. He was at his office and I knew he wouldn't answer the phone. I left a message. I called my parents to find they were not home either. I left them a message as well. I called Cindy. She wanted to celebrate with a bottle of champagne until I reminded her that wasn't a good idea.

"Did you tell him?" she asked.

"About the job?" I said.

"No. About the baby," she said.

"No. I left a message about the job," I said. "I'm waiting until after the wedding."

Steven called me at home that night. I slept through the phone call. He told me he had a surprise for me and promised to call me again tomorrow. "I love you. Don't forget to make your appointment for your check up."

I was busy transitioning at work. Michelle had walked out after her being told she didn't have the job and hadn't come back. I was doing her job and mine as well as setting up things for January. I missed Steven's call at work, but was surprised to find flowers waiting for me on my desk. I was still afraid to call him. I left him another message at home.

He called me again that night, but I had fallen asleep immediately when I got home from work. I woke up at ten and listened to his frightened message. He was insistent I call him on his cell. I couldn't bring myself to do it. We were on a noon flight from Logan the next day. The plan had been for him to meet me at the hospital and we would take a cab from there. I packed my things for the flight and was about to crawl into bed exhausted when there was a knock at the door.

I opened it to find a worried Steven.

"Why didn't you call me?" he said. He was angry. "I've been worried about you."

"I'm sorry," I said. "I fell asleep. I just finished packing everything and all I wanted to do was sleep. I would have called you in the morning."

"At home again?" he said angrily. "Why are you avoiding me?"

"Steven," I said. "I'm tired. Michelle quit yesterday with no notice. I've been doing the job of two people. I still don't feel well. Can we have this discussion later?"

"Fine," He said angrily. "Do you want me to go with you tomorrow?"

"Yes," I said, "but I told you I need time."

"I understand," he said. But he didn't understand. "Do you want me to leave?"

"No, I just want to go to sleep." I pulled his hands. "Can you hold me?"

"Yes," he said. We climbed in bed together. He pulled me up against him. He had his hand on my stomach and was rubbing it. It was like he knew.

"I love you," he whispered in my ear. "No matter what. Follow your heart, Diana. Follow your heart."

I fell asleep in his arms. I woke up at ten to find him gone. He had left me a note. He needed to go back to North Andover to pack and would meet me at Logan Airport. I quickly got out of bed and showered. I needed to leave soon to make the flight.

I took the T to Logan dragging my bags with me. I made my way to the terminal. I waited for Steven at the terminal. They began to board the passengers. Finally at last call, I saw him running through the terminal. I was worried he wasn't going to come.

"You made it," I said to him. When we checked in I discovered his surprise. He had upgraded us to first class.

"I've never flown first class before," I confessed to him.

"Now that's just a crime," he teased. We settled into first class. He ordered champagne for us. I took a sip to make him happy.

"What's wrong?" he asked frowning.

"Nothing. I don't like champagne." I lied.

"Do you want something else?" He asked.

"No. I'm fine," I said.

"I'm sorry I was late," he said. "It took me a little longer than I thought to get everything done."

We landed in Chicago and made out way to the W Hotel. That's when I found out what else he planned for me. He had scheduled me a massage for me and for my mom. The rehearsal dinner was scheduled for seven. My parents arrived while we were at dinner. They left a note for me at the front desk. We went upstairs and Steven pulled me into his arms.

"You are so beautiful," he said to me. "I missed you this week." He was tearing at my clothes. I was wearing the little black dress he had loved so much from my modeling session. I heard the fabric tear as he finally pulled it off me.

"Move in with me," he murmured against my skin. His mouth was making its way down my neck to my breasts. "Please."

"Steven," I whispered. His mouth was at my belly. He was kissing it and pulling at my pantyhose and underwear.

"I want to go to sleep with you every night. I want to wake up with you every morning." I sat on the bed as he ran his hands up my legs. "I want to make love to you every day."

He was lying on top of me staring in my eyes. "Please," he begged again.

"We'll see," I said as he slid inside me. "I love you."

"I love you too," he murmured. Before I realized it we were out of control and I was clawing at his back. He groaned as I moaned and finally collapsed on top of me.

"I'm glad I didn't schedule a massage for me. I'd have some explaining to do," he said laughing at the new marks on his back. He rolled over and took me with him. He was stroking my back. We fell asleep.

Sometime around eight the next morning I woke up to find Steven staring down at me. I smiled. He leaned down and kissed me.

"I scheduled the massage for you and your mom at ten in here," he said.

"You shouldn't have done that," I said. The W was affiliated with Bliss Spas and it was terribly expensive.

"You deserve it. You've been through a lot lately," he said. "Much of it my fault."

"No it's not," I said. "Your mother is just trying to protect her son."

"It's more than that," he said. "I need to tell you about my mom."

I propped my head on my hand and looked at him. He was serious.

"My mom graduated from Vassar and came home to the summer house on Long Island. My grandfather had hired a young man to work on the grounds. He was working his way through law school. She fell in love with him. By the end of the summer she was pregnant with me. My grandmother was irate. She threatened to cut my mother off without a cent. Unfortunately for my mother, that was all my father cared about. He left and my mother was never the same."

"What about your dad?" I asked puzzled.

"My dad married my mom right after my mom gave birth to me. He couldn't have children and was thrilled to have a son. He loves my mom despite all her flaws. She is very protective of me and everything she gained through her sacrifice. I was thirteen before I learned the truth about my birth. My grandmother told me one night in a drunken rant. My grandfather never forgave her for that. Overnight, I turned into an angry young man. I was determined to be everything they wanted me to be and everything they thought they wanted but with a price."

"I'm so sorry," I said.

"Don't be," he said. "I can't change my past. What I want is a future. I want to be happy. You make me happy. I don't want to lose that."

"Steven…" I began. There was a knock at the door.

"That's probably breakfast," he said getting out of bed. He pulled on his boxers and pants.

He opened the door to find my mother and father standing there. The rooms at the W allowed for semi privacy. I didn't know my parents were at the door until Steven called to me.

"Your parents are here." He said nonchalantly as he walked back into the bedroom. I must have turned white. "Please do not pass out on me now." He brought me a thick white terry cloth robe the hotel had provided. I put it on and went into the other room.

"Hi," I said embarrassed.

My mother came forward and hugged me. She whispered in my ear, "You didn't tell me he was so good looking."

I blushed again. "Hi Daddy." I kissed my parents hello.

Steven walked back into the room with a shirt on.

"Did you get the note at the front desk?" Steven asked.

"Yes. That was very nice of you to arrange for the massage. I really can't accept."

Steven put up his hand. "Consider it a Christmas gift." He turned to my father, "Are you up for breakfast while the ladies have their massages?"

"Sure," my father said.

Steven turned to me and said, "We'll finish this conversation later. OK?"

I nodded. I was finally at the point where I could tell him the truth. He leaned down and kissed me.

"I'll see you later," he said. "Enjoy your breakfast and massage." He kissed my mother's cheek and left with my father.

"Diana," my mother exclaimed, "Is he for real?"

"Pretty much. Lest you think there isn't some huge flaw, his mother is the Long Island version of the Wicked Witch of the West," I told her with a frown.

"Well dear. I'll tell you this much. All mothers-in-law are modeled after the Wicked Witch of the West."

"Who says she'll be my mother-in-law?" I asked.

"I just have a feeling," my mother said with a smug smile.

Chapter Thirty

I left Diana in our suite with her mother. Her father and I walked down to the lobby for breakfast. I had an agenda for the morning. I had well laid plans for the day that began with breakfast.

At breakfast, I sat with Diana's father. It was awkward since we had never met. I felt the need to tell him a little about myself.

"Sir," I began.

"Please Steven, call me John," he said.

"John," I began, "this is hard since this is the first time you've met me."

"It's all right. Diana has spoken very highly of you."

"Thank you sir," I said. "I don't know how much you know about me. I have part of a practice in Lawrence, Massachusetts. I'm also teaching a class in General Biology at Merrimack College this spring."

"Diana mentioned that," he said.

"I plan on staying in the Boston area a long time. Diana was just offered a new position at MASS General."

"I know." He beamed proudly as fathers tend to do.

"Sorry," I said. I was nervous. "Sir, um, John, I love your daughter. I can't imagine my life without her."

He smiled.

"She's been sick the past week," I said. He frowned. "She has an appointment next week to get some tests done. I have a couple of theories about what it could be."

"You don't think it's the Hodgkin's again?" he asked concerned.

"That's worst case scenario," I said. "I'm prepared for that, but I think its something else less life threatening."

"What do you think it is?" he pushed.

I blushed. "It's rather hard to admit it to you, but I think she's pregnant."

He broke into a smile. "I could see why you hesitated. That's usually not something a man wants to tell his girlfriend's father. But Diana is special."

"Yes sir, she is," I agreed. "I'm asking you for permission to marry her."

He was silent.

"She makes me happy. I want to make her happy." I said. "We have some obstacles to overcome. The greatest of them is my mother. But I want you to know that Diana is the most important person in the world to me."

"If this is what she wants, I would be happy to welcome you into the family. Jack speaks highly of you."

"Thank you sir. I plan to ask her tonight."

We returned to the hotel room to greet Diana and her mother decked out in white robes. They looked completely relaxed.

"What time do you have to be downstairs to have your hair and makeup done?" I asked.

"I need to be downstairs at noon," she said.

"It's almost eleven thirty now," I informed her

"Oh my God," she said and jumped up.

"Slow down," I said to her, "they'll wait." She went into the bathroom and showered. Her parents excused themselves. Her father shook my hand at the door and her mother gave me a kiss.

Diana emerged from the shower and put on her clothes. I sat and watched her get dressed. It was something I loved to do.

"You missed your run today," I said to her.

She shrugged. "There are more important things to do today," she said.

"Yes there are," I said to her. I pulled her into my lap before she could walk out the door. "I love you."

I kissed her. She put her arms around my neck and sighed. She was wearing jeans and a white button down shirt. "I don't know when I'll have another moment alone with you tonight."

"We'll find a moment," I said.

She left for her hair appointment. I got in the shower. After showering and shaving I lied down on the bed to watch some football. Obviously, the couple getting married today was not college football fans. I must have fallen asleep. I woke up to see Diana leaning over me. "Wake up sleeping beauty."

I opened my eyes and kissed her. "You look beautiful." Her hair was swept up on top of her head and her make up was not overstated but polished.

"I need to get my dress on and get back downstairs. Can you help me?" She asked.

"Sure. Where is the dress?" I asked. She had begun to remove her jeans. She had on black lace underwear and began to roll on stockings. She fumbled with the garter belt. I came over to her. I knelt in front of her and fastened the stockings. It was one of the most difficult things I had ever done in my life. I stood up after kissing the tops of her thighs.

"Thanks," she said. "I won't ask how you know how to do that."

"I'm better at taking them off," I chuckled. I reached into the closet and brought out the dress. I hadn't seen it yet. It was a long black strapless satin dress. I turned to see her fastening the strapless black bustier that she had worn the first night we went dancing.

"That's really not fair," I said. "I'm going to have to sit in church and watch you on the altar knowing you have the most decadent underwear on underneath that dress."

"Penance," she said.

"I guess so," I said as she slipped on her shoes. She came over to me. I held the dress out for her. She stepped into it and I kissed her again. She turned around and I zipped her dress. She stepped away and went to the dresser. Lying on the top of the dresser were the boxes I had given her for Christmas. She put the earrings in and brought me the necklace and bracelet for me to fasten on her.

"You look stunning," I said. "I'll see you at the church."

"I love you," she said as she left the room.

The wedding was at four with a cocktail hour immediately following. The reception was slated to end at midnight. At the end of the evening, I planned to ask Diana to marry me.

I sat with her parents at the church and then again at the reception. Diana was stuck sitting up on the traditional bridal party dais. Finally she came over to me and asked me to set up the salsa dance. The disc jockey began to play a song. We took the dance floor and began to dance. Slowly others left the dance floor and we became the main attraction. Finally the dance was over. Diana's face was pale. I immediately brought her off the dance floor and sat her down.

"Are you OK?" I asked.

She nodded and then passed out on top of me. Unlike the other times when she was close to losing consciousness, she never actually lost consciousness. I carried her out into the lobby. The headwaiter came over.

"Is there a problem?" he asked.

"Can you get me an ambulance?" I asked. I wasn't taking any chances with her. While Julie had her suspicions about Diana being pregnant, I still couldn't rule out the cancer. Diana regained consciousness.

"Relax," I said to her. "There's an ambulance on the way."

"Steven," she said to me, "please don't do that."

"Too late," I said. "Just close your eyes and rest."

When the headwaiter came back to us, I sent him in to find Diana's parents. They came rushing out to us as the ambulance arrived. They loaded Diana onto the stretcher. I insisted on riding in the ambulance with her and told her parents I would call them in their room when I knew something.

We arrived at the Emergency Room. I explained who I was to the attending physician. He allowed me into her room after examining her. She was lying on the stretcher hooked up to an IV. She was sleeping. I quietly picked up her chart and began reading it. It was there as I suspected. She was almost six weeks pregnant. I smiled. I reached into my tux jacket and pulled out the ring box. I had taken my great-grandmother's ring and had it reset and resized to fit her hand. I had two amythest stone added on either side of the two carat diamond. I slipped it onto her left hand ring finger.

She woke up and looked at me.

"Hi," I said to her.

She licked her lips. "Hi," She rasped, "Can I have some water?"

I poured her a cup of water and brought it to her. She took it in her left hand and drank it.

"What's this?" she said looking at her hand.

"Something I've been saving for the right girl," I said.

Tears began to slide down her face. "Steven," she cried.

"Shh..." I said wiping her tears away. "You're dehydrated. Don't cry. I can't stand to see you cry and right now you can't afford to lose the water."

She nodded her head.

"Was there something you wanted to tell me?" I asked.

"I've decided to not run the Boston Marathon this year," she said.

"Wise decision," I said smiling at her. "Can I ask you another question?"

She nodded.

"Will you marry me?" I proposed. "It's not exactly how I planned it, but I love you and I want you to marry me."

"Why?" She asked.

"Because I don't want to make the same mistake my father made. Because I want to follow my heart." I said tears sliding down my face. "Because I can't live without you."

"I love you," she said crying.

"I love you too," I said. "Anything else you want to tell me?"

"The cancer isn't back and according to Cindy I should play the lottery," she said.

"Why's that?" I asked with a smile.

"Because I've been given two miracles in one lifetime. And doctors only practice medicine."

"Some of us better than others," I said leaning over her to kiss her.

"Steven," she whispered as my lips neared hers, "I'm pregnant."

"Good to know," I said kissing her. "I thought you were just allergic to me. Are you really going to marry me?"

"Yes," she said.

"Why?" I asked.

"Because I want to follow my heart too," she said and I leaned down to kiss her again.

Coming This Christmas:

I Can't Live Without You

¥ ✄

Jacqueline M. Ryan

Chapter One

¥

"Are you ready?" I asked him. I was more nervous than he was. I hated being in church. It always unnerved me.

My brother Jim turned around and smiled. He was in full dress Army uniform. We were in the vestibule of St. Ignatius of Antioch Catholic Church in Yardley, Pennsylvania waiting for the beginning of his wedding. I was his best man.

"I've been ready for this since Thanksgiving last year," he said. Jim met Nasrine, his wife in a bar in New York City the day after Thanksgiving. Little did he know that he would end up working with her for the next three months in Iraq. She was an Air Force Captain while he was a Captain in the Army National Guard and an agent with the Bureau of Alcohol, Tobacco and Firearms.

We walked out of the vestibule and watched Jasmine, his stepdaughter, the flower girl walk down the aisle. She waved to Jim as she went to take a seat with her grandmother. Jen, the matron of honor, Nasrine's best friend from high school, smiled at Jim as she walked down the aisle. She had been the one who made Nasrine go out the night she met Jim. Finally, the back door of the Church opened and in came Nasrine and her father. Nasrine's father was also in full dress uniform. An Army General, he was smiling as he walked her down the aisle. Nasrine's first marriage had been disastrous and he was more than thrilled to be welcoming Jim into his family.

Jim met her at the foot of the altar and smiled down at her. She was beautiful on any given day, but today she was breathtaking. I smiled remembering the night I first met Nasrine. She had on fatigues and had arrived at Jim's house with pizza. I had just finished making some pretty disparaging remarks about the Air Force. She put me in my place pretty quickly. She became a vital part of Jim's life very quickly and when she was wounded in Iraq the whole family held their breath. She recovered and now they were getting married.

They had scheduled the wedding on Memorial Day weekend for several reasons. Both Jim and Nasrine had come close to death while serving in Iraq, but they had lost one of their small squad. By having their wedding on Memorial Day weekend it gave their military friends something to celebrate and then a support group to mourn their friend's loss. It also allowed for our very large family to travel to Pennsylvania to witness the wedding. There were six boys in our family. Jim was the second youngest. With Jim married, I became the lone bachelor. My mother had been a widow for ten years and lived to see her grandchildren. Today's wedding would be an excuse to dote on them. There were now ten in all with Nasrine's daughter Jasmine easily fitting into the family. With Jim married, I was sure to have pressure placed on me by my mom to settle down.

While the church ceremony was elegant, the reception was more Jim and Nasrine's style. They had decided to have a tent reception at my house. When I finished my graduate degree at Vanderbilt University in Nashville, Tennessee, I was recruited by Sunoco to work in Philadelphia. My older brother Mark was already living in the Philadelphia area. Soon, Jim had joined us. As I moved up in Sunoco, I had the money to purchase a piece of property in the area. It had a small cottage and a large barn on it. I worked on the cottage first and was living in that while the barn was being renovated. I had just finished renovating the barn this spring. It had been a huge task that had taken almost five years, but one that I had enjoyed. The barn would allow for most of my family to stay there. It had six large bedrooms as well as a large living area. The cottage would become a guesthouse for people to stay in or to be rented out. Tonight it would be where Jim and Nasrine spent their wedding night.

The cocktail hour was held on the stone patio beside the barn as well as in the large open room on the ground floor. Since most of my family had not seen my house, it was a chance for them to marvel at the accomplishment. While I hadn't done any of the work myself, I had worked with the contractors to pick out things that would be true to the one hundred year old structure. Any flooring or molding that was placed in the house was constructed of old barn wood. While I loved antique furniture, I tried to stay away from antique beds and chairs. At six feet three inches, I was way too tall to try to fit into an antique bed. Weighing over two hundred pounds made me skeptical of antique furniture's ability to hold my bulk. Instead, I purchased many new pieces with a country style or Amish constructed furniture that I accented with antiques.

Before I was to give my speech as Jim's best man, I was approached my mother. She was a petite woman who had not lost any of her spunk in her almost seventy years. She was still in charge of this family. It was amazing to see how she had every single one of us under her control if she wanted it. She kept Jim in line despite the fact that he was a federal agent. She told me what to do despite the fact that I commanded the east coast accounting department of Sunoco.

"Andrew," my mother began, " you do have your speech written down?"

"Yes mom," I said with a smile. It was amazing that no matter how successful you were, your mother could always reduce you to the schoolboy that needs to have his homework checked.

"You're not going to say anything crazy like your brother Mark did?" She asked with a frown.

I smiled. All the brothers pretty much agreed that Mark's best man speech at our brother Brian's wedding was hysterical. He had a little too much to drink before he gave his speech and it turned into a drunken rant. The opening lines were perhaps the funniest. He commented on Michelle's beauty saying she was the second most beautiful woman in the room. The first of course, he had said was his wife Karen. He then turned to Brian and explained the first statement. "Brian," he had said, "that's called sucking up. Get used to it." While we had all laughed, my mother raked him over the coals for being drunk.

"Mom," I said. "I learned from Mark's mistake. Also I know I shouldn't do what I don't want done in return." I said it before I realized it left her an opening.

"And when might James be returning the favor of being your best man?" She said wagging a finger at me. "I'm not getting any younger. And neither are you."

"As soon as I find the right woman," I said. I was saved from further scrutiny by the announcement that we should take our seats in the tent for dinner. I walked my mother to her seat and then waited for the DJ to call me for the toast.

"Ladies and Gentlemen," the DJ announced, "it's my pleasure to introduce the best man, the groom's brother Andy."

The approximately one hundred guests seated under the tent clapped as I made my way over to the DJ. He handed the microphone to me.

"On behalf of the Collins family, I want to welcome everyone to and Jim and Nasrine's wedding." I reached into my pocket and pulled out my speech. "OK. Here goes."

"There are many things I could say tonight that would reaffirm what everyone in this room already knows. Jim and Nasrine are meant to be together. They were destined to be together and today fulfills that destiny. Instead, I would like to share with you Jim's words that began the process of this day coming to existence." I unfolded the e-mail I had received after Nasrine had been wounded.

> The last three days have been surreal. First I must say that I am fine and Nasrine is recovering. Our HUMVEE was hit by an IED three days ago. We lost Sgt. Andrews and I almost lost Nasrine.
> I don't know what I would do without her. I'm finishing my tour without her. She will be returning to the US and I don't know how I will make it through each day without her. She is everything to me. I never

thought I would find a woman that would make me so happy. I listen to other soldiers complain about their deployments. I can't complain. It gave me my life. It gave me Nasrine.

You knew that I loved her before I realized it. I thank you for bringing me to that realization. I should be home in less than a month. I have taken the time to make preparations for her as well as for her daughter Jasmine to move in. Take care of them for me. I've ordered her engagement ring to be shipped to my house. I need to keep it from Nasrine. Please do your best to help keep my surprise for her.

I've got to get back to work. I'm learning more and more Arabic and trying to survive every day without her. I hope you will someday feel the emotions I feel when you see the woman you love walk into a room, smile at you, and tell you she loves you. I have that for the first time in my life and nothing, not war or my own stubbornness will prevent me from being with her for the rest of my life.

I looked up at the crowd. Many people were holding back tears. I turned to my brother Jim and his new wife.

"Jim and Nasrine, I wish you only the best in your new life together. I hope to one day have the happiness I see when I see the two of you together. Congratulations."

The wedding progressed as they usually do. At one point I found myself sitting alone watching the many couples under the tent. I was lonely. For the last ten years, I had done little but work. While I was happy with the outcome, I had a comfortable life with a great house and a pretty full bank account, I wasn't happy. I knew it. I needed a change. I had just been asked to go to Japan for a month in July with Sunoco. I agreed to go but knew that when I came back things had to change. They had to slow down. My gaze fell on Jim in time to see him pointing at me. A tall blond man was headed toward me.

"Andy right?" He said as he sat down at the table. I nodded. He extended his hand. "I'm Ted Mulcahy. I went to college with Jim."

"Sure. Ted," I said remembering Jim's friend from Georgia State. "I hope you're having a great time."

"Without a doubt. My wife and I are on a mini vacation right now. We're living overseas in Japan right now. Jim said you're headed there next month."

I nodded taking a sip of my beer. "I'll be in Tokyo for about a month with Sunoco."

He took a card out of his wallet. "Here's our address in Tokyo. Check to see if Sunoco will get you an apartment. There are always apartments for lease in our building. It would be great to see you while you're over there."

"Thanks," I said. "I'll be sure to give you a call when I know where I am staying."

A petite brunette was making her way over to us. Ted turned and waved to her. "That's my wife Sharon. I'll have to admit she has spent most of the night exploring your house. She's fascinated by it."

I laughed. "If she had seen it when I bought it, she would have run."

"That bad?" Ted asked.

"You have no idea," I said. Sharon arrived at the table. I stood up to shake her hand.

"You must be Sharon," I said.

"Yes," she said. "I have to get this out of the way. I am in total awe of your house. We've been living in our apartment in Tokyo for the last two years with another three years in front of us. I am so jealous."

"Don't be. It took way to long to get it to the condition that is now. I have a photo album of the progress."

"I saw it. Your brother Brian showed it to me. He said you're coming to Japan in a few weeks."

"Yes. I already agreed to call Ted when I arrive," I said.

She beamed. "That's great. You'll love Tokyo."

"I hope so," I said.

Chapter Two

I had forgotten how hot Japan was in the summer. The sweat was dripping down my back as I pulled my luggage behind me from the bus stop up the hill to the apartment lobby. As I walked into the lobby I was greeted with a smile and hello from the doorman. I waved and continued toward the bank of elevators. There was a man standing waiting for the elevator. He had with him a collection of luggage. He was obviously moving in. He was engrossed in a document as he waited for the elevator.

The elevator arrived and I stepped on. I held the door open as the man maneuvered himself and his suitcase, garment bag and briefcase into the elevator. He smiled and thanked me. He pressed floor eighteen, which happened to be my floor and went back to reading the document. I studied him as he stood there reading. He was over six feet tall with a muscular build and dark brown hair. The thing that was so striking about him was his eyes. They were a deep green. He was dressed in khaki pants with a navy golf shirt. On the chest of his shirt was the Sunoco emblem.

At the eighteenth floor, I motioned for him to leave the elevator first while I held the door. He did and smiled at me again.

His smile was brilliant. He momentarily stunned me. He had placed his hand on the button outside of the elevator.

"Are you getting off?" He asked. I was thrilled to hear his American accent. So many times, you run into people in Tokyo who are from the west but find they don't speak English. It dashes your hope of a conversation.

"Yes," I said stepping off and pulling my luggage with me.

"Sorry." I turned left down the hallway toward my apartment. The door was decorated with a welcome home sign. I smiled thinking that Sharon had been here. I walked inside and plopped down on the couch. I picked up the phone and called Sharon.

"Hey girl!" Sharon said as she answered the phone.

"Hi," I said. "Thanks for the sign but it's not going to be home for much longer."

"You got the job!" She yelled. "Oh my god! We have to go out and celebrate."

"Not tonight," I said. "You know how the time change goes. I'll have no idea what time zone I'm in. How about tomorrow?"

"Sounds good. Listen a friend of Ted's just came to town. We'll invite him too."

"Sharon," I warned. Sharon was forever finding some unsuspecting guy to try to set me up with.

"Listen," she said. "I have to go. The kids are killing each other."

"No problem. I have to get some groceries anyway," I said.

"Guess you didn't check the kitchen yet." Sharon said laughing. "I'll talk to you later."

I walked into the kitchen to find a fully stocked refrigerator and closet. She was too good to me. I went into the bedroom and began to pull the clothes out of my suitcase. I began to separate the clothes into piles. I needed to have some things dry-cleaned but I began a wash. I was hot and sweaty from traveling from Philadelphia. I jumped in the shower quickly and decided to grab a coffee downstairs.

I put my wet hair up in a twist and grabbed a light tank top and skirt. I grabbed my purse and headed down to the lobby. Just below the apartment building was a Starbuck's Coffee. It was around four in the afternoon and I made my way down the escalator to the Starbuck's. Outside the Starbucks was a patio that had a few customers lingering. Two Japanese men sat at a table drinking their coffee and smoking cigarettes. Their conversation stopped when I walked through the patio. I went in and ordered a coffee. As I was ordering, in came Mr. Green Eyes. He ordered a coffee and noticed me in the shop. He smiled at me.

"Since it looks like we're neighbors, I guess I should introduce myself," he said. "I'm Andy Collins." He hput out his hand to shake.

"Heather Wilson," I said shaking his hand. He had changed into shorts and a new golf shirt. "First time in Japan?"

"Actually yes," he said. "I didn't expect it to be quite so hot."

I laughed. "August is brutal. If you're still here, invest in a handkerchief," I said pulling out the handkerchief I carried to wipe my brow. It was a local habit that most people fall into once they live out a summer in Japan.

"Thanks for the tip," he said. "Did you just get in today?"

"Yes," I said. "It's a long flight. I came down to get coffee to try to stay awake as long as possible."

"That's what brings me down here too. That and the fact that I have no food in my apartment and find myself completely starved."

"They don't have too much to eat here," I said. "I was actually going to order some takeout and continue doing laundry."

"If I offered to pay would you order me something? I'd even help with your laundry to get a decent meal," he smiled that completely disarming smile.

"You may have a deal. I absolutely hate doing laundry," I said laughing. I took out my cell phone and dialed Wolfgang Puck's restaurant around the corner. "Anything in particular you like or don't like?"

"Not really," he said.

I ordered two of the sets for the day and hung up.

"What's a set?" Andrew asked.

"It's kind of the equivalent of the special but it's more than just a main dish. It usually includes an appetizer and a desert and sometimes a drink," I explained. I thought back to when I first arrived in Japan and didn't know about many of the local things.

"Do you want to grab a table or head up to your apartment to get started on the laundry?"

"We can grab a table. The food should be ready in about twenty minutes. I was joking about the laundry. I do hate to do laundry, but you don't have to help. I actually have a girl that comes once a week to clean the apartment and do some laundry."

"How long have you lived here?" He asked.

"It will be two years next month," I said. "I'm actually going to be leaving in about six weeks. It's time for me to head home."

"Where's home?" He asked after taking a sip of coffee.

"Before or after Japan?" I asked.

He laughed and it was a really pleasant sound. "Start before."

"I'm from Ohio originally, but I was living in Nashville before I moved to Japan," I said drinking my coffee.

"Nashville? I went to school in Nashville. How long were you living there?" he asked.

"I went to school at University of Nashville and then stayed on for six more years before moving to Japan." I really hoped he didn't go to school at University of Nashville. I really didn't want my new life and old life to ever cross paths.

"I went to Vanderbilt University," he explained. "Where's home going to be after you leave Japan?"

"Philadelphia," I said.

He laughed again; this time with much more enthusiasm.

"What's so funny about that?" I asked. I was puzzled.

"That's where I live now," he explained taking out his business card. He handed it to me.

I read it. Andrew P. Collins, East Coast Vice-President of Accounting Sunoco. Philadelphia, PA. I laughed too.

"What's that called when things happen by chance?" He asked.

"Serendipity," I said. "You could say it's six degrees of separation, but that would mean we would have to have friends in common."

"You never know," he said looking at his watch. "Do you think the food's ready?"

"Should be. Do you want to walk up to the lobby? The delivery guy should be there soon." We got up from the table and the two Japanese businessmen again stopped their conversation and watched me walk out of the shop.

"What's that all about?" He asked.

"You don't find very many women in Japan who look like I do," I explained. "Often I catch the Japanese men stopping to stare at me." I was five foot six with a very voluptuous build and strawberry blonde hair. I felt the need to clarify the statement to Andy. "Very few Japanese women have curves. It's one of the few places I feel appreciated. I think I'll miss it in Philadelphia."

Andy laughed and I smiled. I was comfortable with him. That was a big change for me. It wasn't often I felt comfortable around men. There was something about him that put me at ease. We arrived at the lobby as the delivery of food arrived. By the time I unzipped my purse, Andy already had cash out and paid for the delivery.

"You really shouldn't have done that," I said.

"Not a problem. I need to get used to the cash," he said. We walked to the elevator. "You can get dinner next time." At eighteen we both got off the elevator. Walking away from my door was Sharon and her youngest daughter Noelle.

"Hey," he said hugging me. "Welcome back." She pulled back and smiled. "Hi, Andy isn't it?"

"Yes," Andy said. "How are you?"

"You know each other?" I asked.

"Andy's brother went to college with Ted," Sharon explained.

"I think it's official," Andy said. "Six degrees of separation really is true."

I began to laugh as we walked into my apartment.

Made in the USA
Middletown, DE
20 November 2019

79099234R00190